DE SHOOTINEST GENT'MAN

The author and a friend

De Shootinest Gent'man

AND OTHER TALES

By NASH BUCKINGHAM

INTRODUCTION BY
COL. HAROLD P. SHELDON

LYON, MISSISSIPPI
WING SHOOTING CLASSICS

WING SHOOTING CLASSICS

DE SHOOTINEST GENT'MAN
By Nash Buckingham

Published by The Derrydale Press, Inc.
printed August 1997

Inquiries should be addressed to the Derrydale Press, Inc.
P.O. Box 411, Lyon, Mississippi 38645
Phone 601-624-5514
FAX 601-627-3131

ISBN: 978-1-56416-164-2

Printed in the United States of America

The courtesy of

FIELD AND STREAM,

RECREATION,

and

OUTDOOR LIFE

*in permitting the publication
of these stories
in book form
is acknowledged.*

TO IRMA

WIFE AND COMRADE

OF UNENDED YEARS TOGETHER;

AND TO THE MEMORY OF

MY FATHER AND MOTHER

THESE GLEANINGS FROM PLEASANT

YESTERDAYS OUT-OF-DOORS, ARE

DEDICATED WITH ETERNAL LOVE,

ADMIRATION AND RESPECT

TABLE OF CONTENTS

		PAGE
	INTRODUCTION	i.
I.	DE SHOOTINEST GENT'MAN	1
II.	ME AN' CAP'N	15
III.	THE HARP THAT ONCE —	17
IV.	SELL OLE DAN?	37
V.	LOST VOICES	39
VI.	BOB WHITE BLUE, BOB WHITE GRAY	57
VII.	MY DADDY'S GUN	83
VIII.	ALL OVER GAWD'S HEAVEN	85
IX.	WHAT RARER DAY	109
X.	MY DOG JIM	127
XI.	PLAY HOUSE	129
XII.	TO AN OLE CULLUD FREN'	149
XIII.	THE NEGLECTED DUCK CALL	151
XIV.	THOU AND THY GUN BEARER	171
XV.	THE FAMILY HONOR	189
XVI.	A SHOOTIN' PO' SOUL	209
XVII.	THE XIVTH OF JOHN	221

LIST OF ILLUSTRATIONS

THE AUTHOR AND A FRIEND . . . *Frontispiece*

"DE SHOOTINEST GENT'MAN"
The late Captain Harold Money . *facing page* 1

HORACE MILLER . . . . . " " 8

"HO'ACE, WHAT YOU STUDYIN' 'BOUT?" " " 15

JACKSON BOUNDS, AND VICTORIA . " " 88

DUCK CALLS . . . . " " 165

"I KNOW MY JOB," AND FRITZ AND PAT " " 190

HORACE AND THE AUTHOR . . " " 228

AN INTRODUCTION

To The Author and his Book

By Colonel Harold P. Sheldon
(Chief Conservation Officer,
U. S. Bureau of Biological Survey)

It is well that the best of the shooting and fishing sketches by Nash Buckingham have at last been collected into a single volume. Appearing from time to time in the sporting magazines of America, these notable contributions to the literature of our field sports have, for years, delighted a national audience of Mr. Buckingham's fellow gunners and anglers. In this more lasting form, they will afford an equal and even greater pleasure to future generations of Nimrods. For every present sign and portent indicates that we are nearly to an end of the sort of shooting this author portrays.

With an inherited love of sport and great opportunities at his door, it is not strange that Nash Buckingham became one of our best game shots as well as a most skillful and seasoned observer of the habits and habitats of wild birds and creatures. An experienced live pigeon shot and for years possessor of a worthy trap-shooting average, Buckingham profitted through access to gun and shell manufacture that rounded out his natural bent for gunning and its tools. Much has been written of his skill, at upland game, and particularly of his ability at "high ducks" with his now famous 12 Bore Burt Becker magnum. It has been my pleasure educationally, to spend a good many days with him in duck blinds, or behind his dogs after Bob Whites in Tennessee and Mississippi. Elsewhere I have myself written of seeing him bring down a limit of fifteen ducks with seventeen shells. I sincerely doubt if any duck was closer than fifty yards, and the two extra loads were used to second-shot badly winged mallards. I fully concur, therefore, with the comment of no less a shooting personage and critic than Captain Paul Curtis, gun editor of Field & Stream who wrote, in March, 1927: "When a shooter like Nash Buckingham says that sort of thing about a shell, it is time to listen. For Nash makes a practice of shooting at ducks and bringing them down dead with surprising frequency at ranges where I leave off shooting at them. I have shot with him on the Mississippi, and I can say, irrespective of whatever other value he may have to his company, he is the best exponent they could get of what a 3 inch shell is capable of doing in a special magnum gun. I have helped a lot of men kill ducks, and at his special forte of knocking them cold at a distance, he has forgotten more than most of us get a chance to learn. The Nash Buckinghams are scarce."

INTRODUCTION

A natural athlete, Nash Buckingham distinguished himself in football, baseball, track and field events during "Prep" days and Varsity exploits at the University of Tennessee. For years, on a great southern newspaper, he wrote a distinguished column as gridiron and general sports critic. During that period he also became perhaps the most formidable but least publicized of the country's amateur boxers. To these physical attributes and accomplishments, the Gods who have in charge the allotment of human faults and virtues, gave him a deep and fine appreciation of literature, music and that most gracious talent of all — a loyal and understanding heart. The reader may conclude as much from his own perusal of the many fine poetical and descriptive passages appearing in these stories. There is ample evidence in the sympathy with which characters are considered and drawn, that the author, like Abou ben Adhem is one who loves his fellow man whether encountered in evening clothes or poised splay footed on the stern of a ducking skiff with a muddy push pole gripped in toil scarred hands.

While the adventures related herein are those generally associated with the destruction of wild life, yet Nash Buckingham has spent an equal energy and sincerity in efforts to aid development of a practical plan for such conservation and perpetuation. He was selected to head and develop the progressive game restoration (incidentally he is the coiner of that now national term) project of a far-sighted ammunition company into what is today associated industrial endeavor along such lines. He later served four years (1928-32) as Executive Secretary of the American Wild Fowlers, a national group, at Washington, D. C., interested in wildfowl restoration, research and their remedial legislation. Many of his ideas and suggestions for the improvement of conditions and shooting ethics adversely affecting wild life, are to be found in plans and programs now under way by Government and States. But, more effective than all the measures and publicity he has created and helped enact, has been the influence of his own personality in fearlessly fostering a greater respect for the principles of rugged, fair minded, tolerant sportsmanship. After all, the best method of securing converts to one's own faith, if it is a reasonably worthy philosophy, is to practice its precepts as Nash Buckingham has done.

DE SHOOTINEST GENT'MAN

"De Shootinest Gent'man"
The late Captain Harold Money

DE SHOOTINEST GENT'MAN

SUPPER was a delicious memory. In the matter of a certain goose stew, Aunt Molly had fairly outdone herself. And we, in turn, had jolly well done her out of practically all the goose. It may not come amiss to explain frankly and above board the entire transaction with reference to said goose. Its breast had been deftly detached, lightly grilled and sliced into ordinary "mouth size" portions. The remainder of the dismembered bird, back, limbs and all parts of the first part thereunto pertaining, were put into an iron pot. Keeping company with the martyred fowl, in due proportion of culinary wizardry, were sundry bell peppers, two cans of mock turtle soup, diced roast pork, scrambled ham rinds, peas, potatoes, some corn and dried garden okra, shredded onions and pretty much anything and everything that wasn't tied down or that Molly had lying loose around her kitchen. This stew, served right royally, and attended by outriders of "cracklin bread," was flanked by a man-at-arms in the form of a saucily flavored brown gravy. I recall a side dish of broiled teal and some country puddin' with ginger pour-over, but merely mention these in passing.

So the Judge and I, in rare good humor (I forgot to add that there had been a dusty bottle of the Judge's famous port), as becomes sportsmen blessed with a perfect day's imperfect duck shooting, had discussed each individual bird brought to bag, with reasons, pro and con, why an undeniably large quota had escaped uninjured. We bordered upon that indecisive moment when bedtime should be imminent, were it not for the delightful trouble of getting started in that direction. As I recollect it, ruminating upon our sumptuous repast, the Judge had just countered upon my remark that I had never gotten enough hot turkey hash and beaten biscuits, by stating decisively that his craving for smothered quail remained inviolate, when the door opened softly and in slid "Ho'ace"! He had come, following a custom of many years, to take final breakfast instructions before packing the embers in "Steamboat Bill" the stove, and dousing our glim.

Seeing upon the center-table, t'wixt the Judge and me, a bottle and the unmistakable ingredients and tools of the former's iron clad rule for a hunter's nightcap, Ho'ace paused in embarrassed hesitation and seated himself quickly upon an empty shell-case. His attitude was a cross between that of a timid gazelle scenting danger and a wary hunter's sighting game and effacing himself gently from the landscape.

Long experience in the imperative issue of securing an invitation to "get his'n," had taught Ho'ace that it were ever best to appear humbly disinterested and thoroughly foreign to the subject until negotiations, if need be even much later, were opened with him directly or indirectly. With old-time members he steered along the above lines. But with newer ones or their uninitiated guests, he believed in quicker campaigning, or, conditions warranting, higher pressure sales methods. The Judge, reaching for the sugar bowl, mixed his sweetening water with adroit twirl and careful scrutiny as to texture; fastening upon Ho'ace meanwhile a melting look of liquid mercy. In a twinkling, however, his humor changed and the darky found himself in the glare of a forbidding menace, creditable in his palmiest days to Mister Chief Justice Jeffries himself.

"Ho'ace," demanded the Judge, tilting into his now ready receptacle a gurgling, man's size libation, "who is the best shot—the best duck shot—you have ever paddled on this lake—barring—of course, a-h-e-m-m —myself?" Surveying himself with the coyness of a juvenile, the Judge stirred his now beading toddy dreamily, and awaited the encore. Ho'ace squirmed a bit as the closing words of the Judge's query struck home with appalling menace upon his ear. He plucked nervously at his battered headpiece. His eyes, exhibiting a vast expanse of white, roamed pictured walls and smoke-dimmed ceiling in furtive, reflective, helpless quandary. Then, speaking slowly and gradually warming to his subject, he fashioned the following alibi.

"Jedge, y' know, suh, us all has ouh good an' ouh bad days wid de ducks. Yes, my lawdy, us sho' do. Dey's times whin de ducks flies all ovah ev'ything an' ev'y-body, an' still us kain't none o' us hit nuthin'—lak me an' you wuz' dis mawnin', Jedge, down in de souf end trails dis mawnin'." At this juncture the Judge interrupted, reminding Ho'ace severely that he meant when the Judge—not the Judge and Ho'ace, was shooting.

"An' den deys times whin h'it look lak dey ain' no shot too hard nur nary duck too far not t' be kilt. But Mistah Buckin'ham yonder—Mistah Nash he brung down de shootinest gent'man whut took all de cake. H'its lots o' de members hu'ah whuts darin' shooters, but dat fren' o' Mistah Nash's—uummp-uummpphh —doan nevuh talk t' me 'bout him whur de ducks kin' hear, 'cause dey'll leave de laik ef dey hears he's even comin' dis way.

"Dat gent'man rode his nigger jes' lak he wuz er saddle an' he done had on rooster spurs. Mistah Nash he brung him on down hu'ah an' say: 'Ho'ace,' he say,

[4]

'hu'ahs a gent'man frum Englan,' he say, 'Mistah Money—Mistah Harol' Money—an' say 'I wants you t' paddle him t'morrow an' see dat he gits er gran' shoot — unnerstan?' I say —'Yaas, suh, Mistah Nash,' I say, 'dat I'll sho'ly do, suh. Mistah Money gwi' hav' er fine picnic ef I has t'see dat he do m's'ef — but kin he shoot, suh?'

"Mistah Nash, he say, 'uh-why-uh-yaas, Ho'ace, Mistah Money he's uh ve'y fair shot—'bout lak Mistah Immitt Joyner or Mistah Hal Howard.' I say t' m's'ef, I say, 'uummmpphh — huummpphh we-e-l-l hu'ah now, ef dats de case me an' Mistah Money gwi' DO some shootin' in de mawnin.'

"Mistah Money he talk so kin'er queer an' brief lak, dat I hadda' pay mighty clos't inspection t'whut he all de time asayin'. But nex mawnin', whin me an' him goes out in de bote, I seen he had a gre't big ol' happy bottle o' Brooklyn Handicap in dat shell box so I say t' m's'ef, I say 'w-e-l-l-l-, me an' Mistah Money gwi' git erlong someway, us is.'

"I paddles him on up de laik an' he say t' me, say, 'Hawrice-uh—hav' yo'-er- got anny wager,' he say, 'or proposition t' mek t' me, as regards,' he say, 't' shootin' dem dar eloosive wil' fowls,' he say?

"I kinder studies a minit, 'cause, lak I done say, he talk so brief, den I says, 'I guess you is right 'bout dat, suh.'

"He say, 'Does you follow me, Hawrice, or is I alone,' he say.

"I says, 'Naw, suh, Mistah, I'm right hu'ah wid you in dis bote.'

" 'You has no proposition t' mek wid me den?' he say.

"S' I, 'naw, suh, Boss, I leaves all dat wid you, suh, trustin' t' yo' gin'rosity, suh.

" 'Ve'y good, Hawrice,' he say. 'I sees you doan grasp de principul. Now I will mek you de proposition,' he say. I jus' kep' on paddlin'. He say—'Ev'y time I miss er duck you gits er dram frum dis hu'ah bottle—ev'y time I kills a duck—I gits de drink—which is h'it? — Come—come—speak up, my man.'

"I didn' b' lieve I done heard Mistah Money rightly an' I says—'uh-Mistah Money,' I says, suh, 'does you mean dat I kin' hav' de chice whedder you misses or kills ev'y time an' gits er drink?'

"He say—'Dat's my defi,' he say.

"I says —'Well, den — w-e-l-l — den, ef dats de case, I gwi', I gwi' choose ev'y time yo' misses, suh.' Den I say t' m'self, I say, 'Ho'ace, right hu'ah whar you gotta be keerful, 'ginst you fall outa de bote an' git fired frum de Lodge; 'cause ef'n you gits er drink ev'ytime dis gent'man misses an' he shoot lak Mister Hal Howard, you an' him sho' gwi' drink er worl' o' liquah—er worl' o' liquah.'

[6]

"I pushes on up nur'ly to de Han'werker stan', an'
I peeks in back by da' l'il pocket whut shallers off'n de
laik, an' I sees some sev'ul black-jacks—four on 'em—
settin' in dar. Dey done seen us, too. An' up come dey
haids. I spy 'em twis'in' an' turnin'—gittin' raidy t'
pull dey freight frum dere. I says, 'Mistah Money,' I
says, 'yawnder sets some ducks—look out now, suh,
'cause dey gwi' try t' rush on out pas' us whin dey come
outa dat pocket.' Den I think—'W-e-l-l-, hu'ah whar
I knocks de gol' fillin' outa de mouf o' Mistah
Money's bottle o' Brooklyn Handicap!'

"I raised de lid o' de shell box an' dar laid dat ol'
bottle—still dar. I say 'Uuuuummmpp-huuummpph.'
Jus' 'bout dat time up goes dem blackhaids an' outa
dar dey come—dey did—flyin' low to de watah—an'
sorter raisin' lak—y' knows how dey does h'it, Jedge?

"Mistah Money he jus' pick up dat fas' feedin'
gun—t'war er pump—not one o' dese hu'ah afromatics
—an' whin he did, I done reach fo' de bottle, 'cause I
jes' natcherlly knowed dat my time had done come.
Mistah Money he swing down on dem bullies—Ker-
py-ker-py — powie-powie-splamp-splamp-slamp-ker-
splaash—Lawdy mussy—gent'mens, fo' times, right
in de same place h'it sounded lak—an' de las' duck fell
ker-flop — almos' in ouh bote.

"I done let go de bottle, an' Mistah Money say—
mighty cool lak—say, 'Hawrice,' say, 'kin'ly to ex-

[7]

amin' dat las' chap clos'ly,' he say, 'an' obsurve,' he say, 'efn he ain' shot thru de eye.'

"I rakes in dat blackjack, an' sho' nuff—bofe eyes done shot plum out—yaas, suh, bofe on 'em right on out. Mistah Money say, 'I wuz—er-slightly afraid,' he say, 'dat I had done unknowin'ly struck dat fellah er trifle too far t' win'ward,' he say. 'A ve'y fair start, Hawrice,' he say. 'You'd bettah place me in my station, so that we may continue on wid'out interruption,' he say.

" 'Yaas, suh,' I say, ' I'm on my way right dar now, suh,' an' I say to m's'ef, I say, 'Mek haste, nigger, an' put dis gent'man in his bline an' give him er proper chan'ct to miss er duck.' I didn' hones'ly b'lieve but whut killin' all four o' dem other ducks so peart lak wuz er sorter accident. So I put him on de Han'werker bline. He seen I kep' de main shell bucket an' de liquah, but he never said nuthin'. I put out de m'coys an' den creep back wid' de bote into de willers t' watch.

"Pretty soon, hu'ah come er ole drake flyin' mighty high. Ouh ole hen bird she holler t' him, an' de drake he sorter twis' his haid an' look down. I warn't figurin' nuthin' but whut Mistah Money gwi' let dat drake circle an' come 'mongst de m'coys—but aw! aw! All uv' er' sudden he jus' raise up sharp lak' an'—Kerzowie! Dat ole drake jus' throw his haid onto his back an' ride on down—looked t' me lak he fell er mile—

[8]

Horace Miller—"*Ho'ace*," *relator of*
"*de shootinest gent'man*"

an' whin he hit he thow'd watah fo' feet! Mistah Money he nuvver said er word — jus' sot dar!

"Hu'ah come another drake—way off to de lef'— up over back o' me. He turn 'roun — quick lak — he did—an' Ker-zowie—he cut him on down, too. Dat drake fall way back in de willers an' co'se I hadda' wade after 'im.

"Whil'st I wuz gone, Mistah Money shoot twice— an' whin I come stumblin' back, dar laid two mo' ducks wid dey feets in de air. Befo' I hav' time t' git in de bote agin he done knock down er hen away off in de elbow brush.

"I say, 'Mistah Money, suh, I hav' hunted behin' som' far-knockin' guns in my time, an' I'se er willin' nigger, sho, — but ef you doan, please suh, kill dem ducks closer lak, you gwi' kill yo' nigger Ho'ace in de mud.' He say—'da's all right 'bout dat,' he say, 'go git de bird — he kain't git er-way 'cause hits daid as er wedge.'

"Whin I crawls back to de bote dat las' time — it done got mighty col'. Dar us set—me in one en' a-shiverin' an' dat ole big bottle wid de gol' haid in de far en'. Might jus' ez well bin ten miles so far ez my chances had done gone.

"Five mo' ducks come in—three singles an' er pair o' sprigs. An' Mistah Money he chewed 'em all up lak good eatin'. One time, tho',—he had t' shoot one o'

them high flyin' sprigs twice, an' I done got half way
in de bote—reachin' fer dat bottle—but de las' shot
got 'im. Aftah while, Mistah Money say, 'Hawrice,'
he say, 'how is you hittin' off—my man?'

" 'Mistah Money,' I say, 'I'se pow'ful col', suh, an'
ef you' wants er 'umble, no 'count nigger t' tell you de
trufe, suh, I b'lieves I done made er pow'ful po' bet.'
He say, 'Poss'bly so, Hawrice, poss'bly so.' But dat
'poss'bly' didn' git me nuthin'.

"Jedge, y' Honor, you know dat gent'man sot dar
an' kill ev'ry duck whut come in, an' had his limit long
befo' de eight o'clock train runned. I done gone
t' watchin', an' de las' duck whut come by wuz one o'
dem lightnin' express teals. Hu'ah he come — look lak'
somebody done blowed er buckshot pas' us. I riz' up an'
hollered—'Fly fas', ole teal, do yo' bes''—'caus Ho'ace
needs er drink.' But Mistah Money just jumped up an'
thow'd him forty feet—skippin' 'long de watah. I say,
'Hol' on, Mistah Money, hol' on—you don' kilt de
limit.'

" 'Oh!' he say, 'I hav'—hav' I?'

"I say, 'Yaas, suh, an' you ain' bin long 'bout h'it,
neither!'

"He say, 'Whut are you doin' gittin' so col', then?'

"I say, 'I spec' findin' out dat I hav' done made er
bad bet had er lot t' do wid de air.'

"An' dar laid dat Brooklyn Handicap all dat time—

he nuvver touched none — an' me neither. I paddles him on back to de house, an' he come astalkin' on in hu'ah, he did — lookin' kinda mad lak' — never said nuthin' 'bout no drink. Finally, he say—'Hawrice,' he say, 'git me a bucket o' col' watah.' I say t' m' sef', I say, 'W-e-l-l-l — das mo' lak h'it — ef he want er bucket o' watah—nigger—you gwi' SEE some drinkin' now.'

"Whin I come in wid de pail, Mistah Money took offin all his clo'es an' step out onto de side po'ch an' say, 'Th'ow dat watah ovah me, Hawrice, I am lit'rully compel,' he say, 't' have my col' tub ev'ry mawnin'.' M-a-n-n-n-! I sho' thow'd dat ice col' watah onto him wid all my heart an' soul. But he jus' gasp an' hollah, an' jump up an' down an' slap hisse'f. Den he had me rub him red wid er big rough towel. I sho' rubbed him, too. Come on in de club room hu'ah, he did, an' mek hisse'f comfort'ble in dat big rockin' chair yonder — an' went t' readin'. I brought in his shell bucket an' begin cleanin' his gun. But I seen him kinder smilin' t' hisse'f. Atta while, he says, 'Hawrice,' he say, 'you hav' los' yo' bet?'

"I kinda hang my haid lak', an' 'low, 'Yaas, suh, Mistah Money, I don' said farewell to de liquah!'

"He say, 'Yo' admits, den, dat you hav' don' los' fair an' squar'—an' dat yo' realizes h'it?'

" 'Yaas, suh!'

[11]

"He say, 'Yo judgmint,' he say, 'wuz ve'y fair, con-siderin', he say, 'de great law uv' av'ridge—but cir-cumstances,' he say, 'has done render de ult'mate out-come subjec' to de mighty whims o' chance?'"

"I say, 'Yaas, suh,'— ve'y mournful lak'.

"He say, 'In so far as realizin' on anything 'ceptin' de mercy o' de Cote'—say—'you is absolutely non-est —eh! my man?'

"I say, 'Yaas, suh, barrin' yo' mercy, suh.'

"Den he think er moment, an' say, 'Verree-verree—good!' Den he 'low, 'Sence you acknowledge de cawn, an' admits dat you hav' done got grabbed,' he say, 'step up'—he say—'an' git you a tumbler—an' po' yo'sef er drink—po' er big one, too.'

"I nev'uh stopped f' nuthin' den—jes' runned an' got me er glass outa de kitchen. Ole Molly, she say, 'whur you goin' so fas'?' I say, 'doan stop me now, nigger-woman—I got business'—an' I sho' poh'd me er big bait o' liquah—er whol' sloo' o' liquah. Mistah Money say, 'Hawrice—de size o' yo' po'tion,' he say, 'is primus facious ev'dence,' he say, 'dat you gwi' spout er toas' in honor,' he say, 'o' d' occasion.'

" 'I say, 'Mistah Money, suh,' I say —'all I got t' say, suh, is dat you is de king-pin, champeen duck shooter so far as I hav' done bin' in dis life—an' ve'y prob'ly as fur ez I'se likely t' keep on goin', too.' He sorter smile t' hisse'f!

" 'Now, suh, please, suh, tell me dis—is you EVAH missed er duck — any whar' — anytime — anyhow — suh?'

"He say, 'Really, Hawrice,' he say, 'you embarrasses me,' he say, 'so hav' another snifter—there is mo', consider'bly mo',' he say, 'in yo' system, whut demands utt'rance,' he say.

"I done poh'd me another slug o' Brooklyn Handicap, an' say—'Mistah Money,' I say, 'does you expec' t' EVAH miss another duck ez long ez you lives, suh?'

"He say, 'Hawrice,' he say, 'you embarrasses me,' he say, 'beyon' words—you ovahwhelms me,' he say— 'git t' Hell outa hu'ah, befo' you gits us bofe drunk'!"

"Ho'ace, what you studyin' 'bout?"

ME AN' CAP'N

Ho'ace, whut yu' studyin' 'bout,
Settin' up 'longside dat fi'ah,
Catfeesh sizzlin' in yo' skillet,
Grease adrippin' thu' de fryer?

Studyin' 'bout dem yams abakin'
In de ash coals 'gin'st de pot,
Contrivin' vittles f'd' Cap'n
Dished up wid gravy, pepper hot?

Coffee b'ilin, pot apurrin',
Cawnpone brown, he'ah whut I say?
Mix two toddies, strong an' stouter,
Cap'n laks bofe his dat way.

Yaas, suh, dis he'ahs sho' contentmint,
Cookin', waitin' on ma' Boss,
Totin' guns an' diggin' goose pits,
Mind de dawgs an' hol' his hoss.

Holler t'me, say, 'Ho'ace'—'Yaas, suh,'
'Roll out ole nigger, hit a lick.'
An' I yells, 'Brek'fus raidy, Cap'n,
Rise an' shine, suh, eat it quick!'

E'vy so off'n', Cap'n crawl me—
Mad 'bout sump'n', cuss lak sin.
'Damn de luck, hell f'ah an' brimstone;'
Den look eroun' at me—an' grin.

Could'n' be no better boss n' Cap'n,
He trusts dis servant, night or day,
Ef hard times comes, ur sickness in de house,
He'ah whut my Boss Man all'us say—

'Don't yu' worry none, ole nigger,
'Bout yo' rent ur whut yu' owe,
Sen' an' draw yo' meat an' 'lasses,
Call de doctah to yo' do'h —

'Sen' de bill t' Cap'n, Ho'ace,
Git yo'sef all right, an' well,
Huntin' time gwi' soon be wid us,
Les' saddle up an' give 'em Hell!'

Ole nigger's Gawd d' same as Cap'n's,
I tells HIM—'thank yu', SUH, f' dis my fren',
Please mek YO' LIGHT t' shine us to YO' CAMP,
An' le'me serve my Marsters dere, Amen!'

THE HARP THAT ONCE—

*"O, had I known as then, Joy would
    leave the paths of men,
I had watched her night and day, be sure,
    and never slept agen.
And when she'd turned to go, O I'd
    caught her mantle then,
And gave her heart my posies,
    all cropt in a sunny hour,
As keepsakes and pledges, all
    to never fade away."*

JOHN CLARE.

T HE dawn of youth's call afield brought to me our comradeship, and an abiding affection therein for him. Somehow, he seemed to happen rightfully into my life; an upstanding, wholesome man's man, with booming, resonant voice, humorous hair triggers in his keen, tender grey eyes and a heart, God guard his destiny, as big and as staunch as a barn door. His was a soul that will ever ride the crest. To my dear father he was always affectionately "Arthur," and Dad to him was "Miles;" and their tracks ranged trail side by side. So, for their being at heart but overgrown boys, beyond the supreme command of Dad's flag, Mister Arthur became by that vaguely intuitive but emphatic diagnosis of boyhood, my ally, confidant and hero. And now that almost forty years have ranged their axe marks along a trail he began blazing into game restoration's tangled wilderness, how splendid it is to look about the clearing and realize that the ethics he visualized and fostered and fought for, have definitely become a louder and clearer watchword of an organized unity of outdoor clansmen. There was but one Mister Arthur —"Guido," whose facile pen traced frost upon the pumpkin, helped pioneer American field trials, and lived, unselfishly, incomparable joys of the chase.

In the period of which I write black powder was but sensing encroachment of a smokeless product. Repeating shotguns were tricky novelties. Autoloading weapons were mere dreams of a Jules Verne vintage. Our old fashioned street was almost out in the country in those days. Mister Arthur and Miss Laura were next door neighbors; their antebellum home set well back among oaks, maples and magnolias. It was approached along a square-bricked promenade hedged with ground-sweeping cedars beautifully interspaced with magnificent hollyhocks. Miss Laura, all in white and a charming picture of wifely devotion, knits amid the shady aloofness of a vast, broad columned veranda. To me that playground is a life memory of droning bees, busy humming birds and scents of mingled rose and honeysuckle.

Down in the wood's lot was Mister Arthur's kennel. In those days gentlemen, for the most part, trained their own shooting dogs, and to the queen's taste, too. *Whip*, forerunner of the mighty *Gladstone*, had gone the way of all dogflesh. But *Gladstone* himself belonged to another of our neighbors. Many an afternoon I've romped and chased squirrels amid the convent's oaks with the old cuss. Like Julia O'Grady or the Colonel's lady, he was, down under the skin, just plain "dawg," and a good fellow among boys. Mister Arthur's full gun dog string was a variegated assortment of bird and water canines, with hounds and beagles thrown in, aristocrats and *canaille* of such breeds. No hungry stray, however, was ever chased away unfed, provided, of course, he dared the mob and fought his way gamely to the potlicker. By right of might certain dogs achieved and held rank against all comers. I've spent whole afternoons searching for and dragging puppy scions from beneath cobwebby house-sills. And evenings, figuring pedigree papers and choosing names for future challengers to title in pointer and setter Halls of Fame. Many a night, lodging with some crony urchin at Mister Arthur's, we fought field trial winners for a fair share of bed covers. Naturally I came by a great fondness for dogs and guns. How Dad did love the game, too. He lost no opportunity to indulge his sons. Here's looking toward him — and Mister Arthur!

Even now, with almost that moment's same acute thrill, I recall the momentous occasion of our first shotgun, a light, sixteen bore Parker double with hammers, given us at Christmas. It was, I am sure, the most wonderful gift ever handed two joyous, speechless lads — with a snow clad world outside. 'Ere nightfall hare gore stained the pallid heath. I was too wee to make bold with the piece, but of sufficient stride to accompany "Bubber" as official admirer and game bearer. For a season I was content to keep up with him, burdened with a sugar-sack game wallet that gained the weight of multiplied mill stones with the addition of each victim. Soon my achieving proportions warranting a share of shots, sounded need for another weapon or a resort to fisticuffs. So from some blessed avenue I became owner in fact of a bourgeois twelve bore, the work of an obscure Britisher. Though for me a heavy, clumsy fowling piece, with flaring, donkey-eared hammers, it shot a smooth, strong pattern. But above all, by that immeasurable standard of faith and reliability, t' was mine own.

And oh! those pioneer Bob White hunts when I first followed Mister Arthur and Daddy. We rose long, long before daylight in those autoless times. We drove for hours through star-tented darkness and softly graying, frost quilted dawns. Bubber and I and the dogs huddled for warmth beneath a buffalo robe. What tummy-stuffing breakfasts in some friendly farm house, as lamp and candle light paled when the sun shot his spangled headpiece over our campaign country. Breathless thrills at the first covey find; glowing health unfolding with each moment. Lunches spread upon log tables by creek banks; wagers laid upon each day's bag. Supreme tenseness when a missed bird meant victory or defeat. Such tired little lads at day's end, invariably snoozing on the way back to town. Sweetest of all was home-coming. For Mother was always waiting; anxious, blessed Mother, with kisses, sugar-butter biscuits, tea and jam, for all parties concerned. Two bold but tired young gunners rarely ever remembered being tucked into dreamland.

Friday nights, in winter time, we youngsters were taken to a duck club to which father and Mister Arthur belonged; a preserve of some five thousand acres of lake, riparian tracts, and virgin timberland, bought for a song. In those days it was gossiped rank extravagance to pay as much as a hundred dollars for a membership in any gunning organization. But now their little old log cabin stronghold is a concrete mansion, and hemmed with private lodges, to boot. With a little encouragement today's shareholders would dress for dinner, and as to sentiment,— deponent saith not. God save the mark! In early days there was no bag limit. As a matter of fact, the coming of that duck club displaced free-shooting market hunters who shipped thousands of wild fowl to northern markets annually. Mister Arthur clamped on a limit of fifty ducks per day, a high figure to look back upon. Later, through his demand, this was materially reduced. The only limit that remains is Uncle Sam's present fair and necessary figure.

What jolly nights those Old-Timers had. How they loved their weapons and every detail of gunning. The first repeating shotgun I ever saw was a Spencer, operated by Mr. Bonnie, a famous shot from Louisville, Kentucky. But for the most part our fathers clung to works of art by Greener, Scott, Smith and Westley Richards. They believed in stiff powder loads, plenty of big shot, and devil take the recoil. They made an early start for their blinds, worked like Turks for their game when need be, and took toddy as often as they frequently felt so inclined. Sterling shots they were, too. Taintless of porcine streak or sweat dodging. We lads were kept well at heel, and were warned to talk short unless otherwise bidden. Wretched the youth who blabbed of how many "snorts" Mister So-and-So took. Or how much changed hands in the poker game we peeped at from a sheltered observation post around the chimney corner. Some of those mornings are priceless memories. At the entrance to Big Lake, for instance: the sun's curtain of fire enfilading trenches of jagged skyline; filmy cypress tops etched against blue satin; countless thousands of ducks booming from spray flung wave jets! Swan gangs blaring gangway! Clanging files of disturbed geese, muffling the drum-fire of one's pulse.

On any hunt Mister Arthur was the life of the party. His locker at Wapanoca, or trunk at Beaver Dam, literally a gunner's treasure trove to a boy. He preferred having us lads help him paw over old shells and hunting gear which he tumbled promiscuously from his helter-skelter plunder abodes. He rarely joined the poker game, but told us stories of his boyhood home in the hill country; tales of bear and deer hunts with his Civil war body-servant, Landom Harris, handling the strike dog and packs. I can see Mister Arthur right now. Begirt in a stained dressing robe, and, from a rocking chair just off the huge fire-place, punctuating the dramatics of recital with flourishes of his glass of heady punch. A ring of intent little faces drinking in the thrills of the battles and death of his two greatest hounds, Rambler and Bugler Ben, slain together in mortal combat with a gigantic panther. We usually slept three in a bed after that yarn. Once in a while some reference was made to his own son who had died a mere shaver. We always wanted to hear more about him. But somehow when Mister Arthur started on that, a wistful shadow settled about his fine eyes, and off he branched into hair's breadth forays and brushes with the Yankees. Ofttimes our dreams, reeking with powder smoke and saber charges, to say nothing of too much supper, took a nightmarish turn. But in moments of quiet in his office, when he let business slide to write gunning essays for the few outdoor publications of that day, Mister Arthur, like some men, had a favorite tune which he whistled or hummed during particularly happy interludes. His was that old Irish lay, "The Harp That Once Through Tara's Halls." He rarely ventured beyond its first line or two before branching off into "Old Dan Tucker" or "Annie Laurie." But all in all "The Harp That Once—" was his heart's melody.

Then, just as the glory of October days gathered for the first shock of killing frost and made it high time to begin decoy painting, the crash came. One evening, home from the bank, father was very grave and not quite himself. After supper he and Mother talked alone in the library, while we boys, a most extraordinary proceeding, were sent upstairs for lessons. Mister

Arthur and Miss Laura called and it was past midnight when we heard them leave. Next evening a similar conference occurred, with lawyers present. Mister Arthur had grown suddenly haggard. Mother spent much of her time at Miss Laura's, and three days later father informed us that our neighbors were going out West to live. There was talk of a will, a relative's deed, heavy endorsements and suspicion — terms wholly impenetrable to children other than their terrible import of parting with Mister Arthur. Real estate agents tacked "For Sale" signs upon his oaks. Vans bundled off loads of priceless furniture. The shooting dogs, one by one, disappeared mysteriously. All we sensed was that direful misfortune had befallen our hero. But he laughed at us as of old. Made jests of his leaving and how he and Miss Laura would come home from Texas with a cattle fortune. I heard father tell Mother that "chickens would come home to roost and a day roll around when Arthur would be vindicated before the world." Whatever that meant, I believed and remembered it, knowing Dad.

Came pangs of farewell. When the carriage came to carry Mister Arthur and Miss Laura to the depot, my hero, leading Barney his favorite and famous setter, and carrying his imported double bird gun, came striding up our driveway. When Dad and I met him, he said, "Buster, here are Barney and the old gun for you.

I want you to have and keep them all for your very own — to remember me and our good old times by — I know you'll take care of them — and — and — always try to live like a good, clean boy." But he sorter choked up and had to turn away. Father cried out, "Arthur — Arthur — my dear fellow," and, putting an arm about his shoulder turned him away. While I, with my whole world black and crumbling, burst into tears and walked back along the rose hedge, leading Barney and sobbing as though my heart would break.

For many, many moons the gap lay wide and deep. Lad that I was, I never saw Barney on a point, or cocked an eye down that treasured gun's rib, without thinking of Mister Arthur. Many an enthusiastic letter I penned to my old friend; of my hunts, school progress and how much I missed him and Miss Laura. Invariably he replied promptly, telling me of the great new country, its wide plains, hard work, buoyant life and game resources. School days swept into college years. Barney passed on, but remnants of his noble blood sprinkled down the lists of field trial champions. Dad heard off and on from Mister Arthur, while Christmas seasons brought affectionate little tokens and pledges of gentle faith. Thus nearly twenty years sped away. Then, as abruptly as came that thunderbolt of earlier days, my father's prediction came true. A sinning relative's death-bed confession righted a great wrong done Mister Arthur. The fields of his forebears, estates and holdings, swept away by false signatures, were his again. And for the first time I discovered that it had been Dad who stood by Mister Arthur in his hour of need and staked him west until a fresh start could be made and the debt be slowly but meticulously repaid. Mister Arthur's response to the good news was characteristic. He and Miss Laura would close out their holdings at the earliest moment possible and return.

A better story teller than I should describe that re-union. I remembered Mister Arthur as above six feet, a wedge-shaped chap with a thatch of thick brown hair. He could ride as only one of Bedford Forrest's cavalrymen had to fork a horse. And Lord! how he could shoot. At last they were home! Miss Laura, but for her silvered locks and "specs," the same beauty. And Mister Arthur? Brown thatch a white mane. Broad shoulders a bit sagged. But tender grey eyes still at hair trigger, and his deep voice still vibrant. Beyond repressed emotion, and a necessary discussion of the important business in hand, a main phase of Mister Arthur's visit bore upon quail shooting prospects. I told him everything I could recall of lapsed years, but, when I put back into his hands that handsome bird gun he had given me so long ago — still a flawless tool — the old gentleman all but broke down. He shrank perceptibly from any vestige of publicity. He would fancy, he allowed, "slipping away with you on an old time bird shoot and, incidentally, a scouting trip around my old diggings."

Next afternoon a local train set us down in the gloam of a December day at his old home town. It seemed strange that I, who, as a mere lad, had followed this man afield in the days of his power and glory, should return with him after so many years of denial and hardship, but with his feet set once again upon a better road down the far slope. As though he had been gone since but yesterday, he turned toward where the tavern ought to be. Trudging a shaded Main Street of summer, but now gaunted into sere oaks and sycamores, toward Court House square, he pointed excitedly to spots from yester-youth. Yonder he had gone to school — where that tumbly brick building stands; there old man So-and-So had kept a trading post — over that way, across the hitching lot, his company had formed and ridden away to the Civil War. Names leaped to memory; gonfalons arrayed themselves company by company. But no one recognized in us any part of a sensation that had previously racked a countryside. At the old fashioned livery stable we arranged for a double rig and two saddles. We breakfasted by lamplight, just as we had done so many times before. And again a jolly sun stole up and set village roofs asmoke with frost mist.

I was proud of my dogs, Jimmy and Don. Fit for even Mister Arthur to pull a gun over. We clattered the rig up hill and down dale. From a scrub oak ridge a wonderful valley opened, with river bottoms in the distance. Crossing those Mister Arthur showed me where, as a laddie-buck, he had potted his first wild ducks. His delight knew no bounds, he was young again, searching for landmarks, clucking and sighing with disappointment when some memoried vantage point failed to materialize. Recalling folks from his old days hereabouts, he wondered if, by any chance, any of them could still be alive. Knowing the lay of the land so well, Mister Arthur finally drew reins at a crossroad, suggesting we saddle up and hunt 'cross country the rest of our way. A farmer gladly ran our conveyance under his shed. At a fence gap Mister Arthur turned into a vast expanse of sedge, post-oak and pine islands. Jim and Don had long since been whipping off their wire edges. Now, far ahead, they were cutting up respective territories; the noble setter's feathered plume switching merrily. Don's black and white showed clear cut as he raced a brambled bench. Mister Arthur sat his horse like a knight of old. My heart leaped for joy. At that moment he was nearly seventy-five years young.

Suddenly Mister Arthur, watching keenly, tossed aloft an arm — "P-o-i-n-t!" Three hundred yards away, where a mock orange row whittled off downhill to meet a belt of ragweed, Don, striding full blast, endeavored frantically to check, turned sidewise and slid into as stylish a point as any bird dog ever contrived. Jim, catching his pal's curved posture, honored it a hundred feet away. No mounted skirmisher ever quit his steed with the graceful alacrity of Mister Arthur's departure from that livery stable nag. He might have been taking cover from a hot corner in cavalry days. Opening his old gun, he fumbled the flap-pocket of his faded corduroy coat, produced two shiny red shells and walked crisply toward Don. The Lord was gracious, I said to myself, to have spared us both this moment. No admonition as to shooting positions, right or left, was needed. Hadn't he raised me? The very humor of anyone's, much less myself, telling Mister Arthur where or how to shoot Bob Whites! In he walked.

With a dynamic buzz and swirl, a bevy exploded just beyond Don's pop eyed stare. I couldn't shoot; I just had to watch Mister Arthur. Could he "come back?" There it was again! The same fractional pause; then up came his weapon — hitched quickly, but steadily. His eyes handled the covey, the gun itself. A husky cock-bird, skimming the briars for an opening higher up, wilted at the fringe of mock-orange and tumbled into the weed tops. A second fugitive, arcing over sassafras tippets, quartering a rush for life that ended just short of the skyline, was sent hurtling. A clean, beautiful double. Would that I could see him right now — just as he stood there! Boot tops flipped with frost dribble from the sedge. Stained, bottle green shooting coat sharp against the brilliant sunlight. Hair and moustache clear marble against his weatherbeaten tan. "My boy"— there was an excited quaver in his voice, "my boy, I'm a very, very lucky old dog; I have made a sure enough, old time double." And while I was lying right prettily as to why I hadn't done a share of shooting, in came Don and Jim, each trying to nuzzle a bird into my old friend's trembling hands. I consider that moment one of my life's really great reunions. Then second nature called us into pursuit of singles. Down a branch bottom, where escaping birds had straggled into tangleweed and blackberry bushes, first Jim and then Don gave exhibitions. A few turns at such, and we were again in the saddles. A few wide casts and three or four more covey finds were behind us. Thick woods and creek beds; acorns crunching beneath horses' hoofs, the spice of herbs and acrid tang of dying timber in our receptive nostrils. At noon, still a few miles, Mister Arthur said, from his old plantation, we made a happy meal. Jim and Don nosed their fair share, and rolled for a siesta in beds of warm leaves. We followed suit, a field custom Mister Arthur hadn't forgotten. With saddles for pillows and our slickers and saddle blankets for cover, we napped.

I wish you had been with us that afternoon. You, too, could easily have downed your limit. You would have followed us across plateaux rich in peas and hollows sweet with sorghum. Everywhere, daggers of corn were driven into cotton lowlands. And how those dogs of mine did handle the birds. Late afternoon brought us to the rim of a bluff overlooking a considerable stream that Mister Arthur called Big Black. "Yonder," said he, pointing to a chalky bluff, "at the foot of that lower knob, I learned to swim — so did my brothers and Landom Harris — the whole countryside, for that matter. Ed Daniels was drowned there, too, and for a long while we wouldn't venture in." Fording the river at a crossing well remembered by Mister Arthur, we trotted a worn bridle path skirting the clear, green water. Atop a commanding ridge we came suddenly upon an old double log cabin, it's "dog-trot" sheltered with vines and hung beneath with gourds and red pepper strings. A bundle of fishing canes leaned against the eaves. A freshly killed hog, with turkeys and chickens in the background, told a story of plenty. Cur dogs and hounds gave us noisy welcome and a fat colored woman answered our hail. Silencing the din, she herded behind her a bunch of pop-eyed pickaninnies and came toward us, grinning welcome.

"How do you do," said Mister Arthur; "what is your name?"

"Angeline Downs, suh."

"Have you lived around here long, Angeline?"

"Yas, suh, Cap'n; I wuz borned right back o' de big house up yonder — Landom Harris is my Gran' papa, suh!"

Mister Arthur started, almost violently. "Landom Harris — your grandfather — he — he — is — alive then — why — you are fairly well along yourself, woman, and I figured Landom long since dead." But Angeline reassured him.

"He ain' daid, Cap'n, but he's mighty ole — he's in yonder now — settin' by de fi'ah — but he fishes er little an' gits aroun' tol'able."

Off his horse and into the dog-trot stalked Mister Arthur, with Angeline and me following. In a spacious, low-ceilinged room, spotlessly clean with two four-poster beds mere islands in its expanse, sat an old grizzled negro, close to a cherry log fire. His wrinkled face wore an air of resigned placidity, almost as though he listened, or tried to read in the flames memories from long ago. Mister Arthur went quietly up to him and said, "Landom!" The veteran lifted his gaze, and, without a word, looked long and earnestly. "Landom," repeated my companion, "you don't remember me — I am — Mister Arthur, Landom."

Gradually, as reason fought its battle with the years, understanding came. Landom's eyes slowly blinked full of tears, and his lips moved, inarticulate. Seeking to rise, his hickory cane beat a tattoo as he struggled up to attention. He knew now, just as Mister Arthur had looked past the mask of infirmity and seen a stalwart slave riding with him to the wars again. Then the storm broke. Their hands went groping to clasp in as honest and heartfelt affection as God's hearts ever feel. The slave's hoary head bent slowly upon his old master's sleeve. And Mister Arthur's arm went round those bent shoulders. How long they clung thus I cannot say. I remember crossing quietly to the cavernous fireplace and looking down into the flames until my own eyes dried.

It would, I vow, be pure romancing to prolong this story — a plain little true story of the quail fields. It is told now — almost. Under Angeline's guidance, Mister Arthur and I rode on to the Big House, a vast pile of brick, ivy growth, white columns and melancholy. An ensemble of pre-war grandeur long lost in gloom and given over to some sleepy caretaker. The last named, awed in the presence of his new master, showed us through. Our footsteps rang hollow through wide halls and lofty chambers. Dusty portraits of gentlefolk in ball gowns and regimentals looked austerely upon us. Musty gloom hung heavily over the premises.

"Sleep here?" replied Mister Arthur, "not this night, my boy." He headed for Landom's cabin. We supped at the old slave's bounteous table; off country ham, fried rabbit, hot biscuits and a sweet potato pie. Long, as long goes to tired hunters, we sat by the fire. Mister Arthur and Landom went back together across storied years. They swam under the chalk bluff and hunted grounds that had been lost but were now found again. They "re-jined" the cavalry, and once again "tented tonight on the old camp ground." Angeline smoothed our beds, and moved Landom and the "picks" into a room across the dog trot. From there, later, I looked out upon night frost and our string of Bob Whites hanging high against the moonlight. The note of a running hound mellowed the distant bottoms. Was it not, I asked myself, the Master of Game, who wrote: "Now shall I prove how hunters live in this world more joyfully than any other men. For when the hunter riseth in the morning and he sees a sweet and fair morn and clear weather and bright; and he heareth the song of the small birds the which sing so sweetly with great melody and full of Love each in his own language in the best wise that he can, according that he learneth of his own kind. And, when the sun is risen, he shall see fresh dew upon the small twigs and grasses, and the Sun, by HIS virtue shall make them shine. And that is great joy and liking to the Hunter's

[35]

heart." Truly, we had had HIS proof, that day.

Through the door of our room I glimpsed Mister Arthur. He was seated in front of the fire, removing his boots and crooning softly — "The Harp That Once—"

—SELL OLE' DAN?

Naw, suh, dawgs ain' dawgs no mo',
Y' see I've owned a sight o' them —
Bred 'em, raised 'em, fooled an' cussed 'em,
Fed 'em when I wuz th' po'est critter
On th' whol' dad-busted farm m'se'f —
Nursed th' sick an' buried dead 'uns,
Som' good, som' bad — all kin' o' dawgs —
That is, meanin' huntin' dawgs.
I ain' never had no time
F' none o' these he'ah fancy pests
Like chows an' poms an' toys,
Gim'me a dawg that hunts som' kin' o' game,
Birds, r' rabbits, ducks r' squirls,
A ramblin', man's size, goin' dawg,
Beagle, deer or fox hound — shucks —
Jus' so he hunts an' fights an' makes a noise.
Som'times I gits t' thinkin' 'bout ole dawgs
Back home whin I wuz jes' a lad,
Mister, you don' see no dawgs like them t'day,
Makes a fella feel jes' sorta' sad.
Y' take ole Jim-dawg,
Er thet ole' cross-bred dropper, Dan,
I raised thet flee-bit puppy on a bottle, say,
All dawg, he wuz,— thar wuz er Man.

SELL OL' DAN?

Y' never seen ole Dan afoolin' 'roun
Whar birds wuz liable not t' be;
Why Dan, he'd bark when he wuz on er p'int,
An' call y' to him — hope t' die he would,
I've see'd him p'int a bird up in a tree.
Don't go, Mister, hones', lis'sen he'ah,
Retrieve?
Why say, ole Dan wuz darn nigh human —
Hones', I got home one night an' counted out m' birds
An' foun' thet one o' them had got away —
Ole Dan jes' shook his haid, all puzzled lak,
But rambled off an' fetched it back, nex' day —
Thet's t' kin' o' dawg Dan wuz — say —
Wait er minit, lis'sen, Mister,
One time er fella' says t' me says
'Lis'sen, how erbout' er hun'nerd dollars cash f' Dan?'
But I jes' looked him squar'ly in th' eye
An' smiled, an' says 'Mister you don't really mean
T' think I'd sell ole Dan f' cash — in han'?'
An' he says 'Yep,' but I jes' giv' another smile
An' says, why, Mister, you've sho' done bought
Yo' sef a dawg, er hun'nerd dollars CASH?
Why, Mister, hell a mile.'

LOST VOICES

T HE tos and fros of livelihood take me about our old
city quite a bit. As with most of us so occupied, even
where one has "grown up," there are districts which
get away from one; neighborhoods which rarely call.
Upon such summons, I find myself looking about curiously for landmarks; keenly receptive to impressions
and reflective associations which, in turn, start trends
of ripening recollection. We'll say then that I have
gone a good long piece north on our Main Street; far
past where skyscrapers and more pretentious marts
whittle off into blocks of dingy, scraggly "cribs;" a
quarter of drowse and lethargy, unabashed commercial
tawdriness and unkempt confusion. Fashion has faded
into obvious and olfactory fustiness. Pawn shop windows, trashily and seductively aglitter, rub elbows with
smelly cobbling hutches; the tin-panny ding-chatter
of aphidian syncopation brazenly summons colored
denizens from "Hot Cat" eating stands to the sanded
platforms of electrified jazz and its altar and burnt

offerings of "snack house." Camouflaged by tonsorial
frontages in casual confab, musk, lather and "hair
straightener," the dulcet click of pool balls and guarded finger poppings of pleading crapshooters, combat
strident cries of street urchins stamped for the most
part as to racial issue with Russo-Hebraic mintage
from skim off the melting pot.

I stop at a cobblestoned alley leading westward down
to the Canal. Greasy-currented Wolf River eddies
emulsions of civilization into the mighty Mississippi.
I easily pick up landmarks. A shabby, out-at-the-
elbows resort crouching shamefacedly behind its "For
Rent" signs. The other, patched and bulgy with tell-
tale sag of impending dissolution, still doing business
as a hide warehouse. Yes, in and around this district
lay original Memphis, trading post and Indian en-
campment. Here, strangely enough, my maternal
grandsire shared the friendship and hospitality of
"Billy," a Chief of the Chickasaws. And hereabouts,
too, from a forlorn cavity of those "For Rent" signs,
came my first meeting with two noble hunters whose
lost voices ring back across memoried currents that
swept them from primal strongholds. With them in
mind and thrilled by passages from the script-like
memoirs of grandfather's stay at the fourth Chickasaw
bluff, it is easy to sweep from Memphis every vestige
of its saw-toothed, smoky skyline of civilization and

picture its eminence a pawn upon the board of conquest.

Visualize with me the gorgeous standard of Spain showered with arrows! De Soto's barge builders of 1541 disputed passage by war canoes of the Arkansas! Conceive brooding silence of a hundred and thirty-two years ere the coming of Marquette and the Sieur de la Salle! What of Bienville and Iberville — brothers dreaming of a mighty empire to lay at the feet of France? And D'Artaguette! Again a surge of war pirogues as his motley army of Choctaws, renegades, negroes and northern Indians scale the bluffs and strike cross country for an assault from the rear upon beleaguered Chickasaws. Utter rout and death at the stake for that gang! Not far from where I, too, stand dreaming, the lilies and tri-color of France floated from Fort Assumption, its guarded ramparts ashake with the growl of the British bulldog hot upon the scent of domain and eager to be at grips! Intrigue and treaty! Dishonor upon honor, white minds and white hands forever fastening a throttle upon red throats! Boone's Long Hunters have come and gone; the bones of Revolutionary patriots and seekers of the Rainbow's End lie bleached or buried beneath the loam of game-infested prairies that lipped to the very brink of the bluffs. Last treaties have been signed! Descendants of those Chickasaws with whom my grandfather smoked the

pipe of peace as their maidens swayed through gyrations of their Sun Dance, have signed away last vestiges
of territorial right and retreated toward the setting sun
and segregation, ignominious, inevitable—deathless!
Another shift of years and the raucous blast of steamboat whistles proclaims conquest of a mighty current
and birth of organized commerce! Yet another lapse
for civil strife, war canoes sheathed in steel and grinning with great ordnance; bluffs shaken to the roll of
battle locked monsters whose ribs and keels and crews
are mouldering hulks in the silt depths! Cannons of
the blue and mortars of the gray now dream away the
years in Peace! Old friends, old faces, old voices—are
they really lost?

I'd best tell you about the Professor first. Time was
when that old hide warehouse was our only theatre. It
isn't difficult or unpleasant to hark back more than
thirty years! I remember going there with Dad and
standing in what he called the rotunda, a sort of crystal
maze lit with flaring, reflecting gas jets. I held very
tightly to Dad's hand while he bought tickets of the
painted faced gent with a false nose who peeked out of
a cubby-hole. The seats were stiff and creaky, but the
subdued red glow of the footlights; the romance and
glamour and appeal to childhood's wondering, gushing
eagerness brings me catch-breath at the recollection!
Perched above the band or orchestra or "the musi-

cians" sat the Professor, a rugged, towering leader whose white flowing hair framed a broad kindly countenance. I can see his bow rise and fall in appealing beats and imperial summons when the brass responded in a crashing climax of drum and cymbals. Salvini! Barrett! Irving! Modjeska! And when Mister Joseph Jefferson—not Jefferson—but a real Rip Van Winkle and his dog, were driven out into the storm, I buried my face in Dad's great coat and burst into tears.

We were just getting up from breakfast at our duck club Waponoca one morning—it wasn't daylight by a "long-shot" when they took coffee and ham and eggs in those old days—when the door banged open and in strode my music master, the Professor. Dad set me to help him unwind some tangled decoy strings and weights, and that's how I really met him; he didn't fuss at me a bit. After that time he let me go with him in his boat once in awhile. He led the band at night; went to the railroad yards after the show; crawled into the caboose of a freight train crew he was friendly with, snatched a bit of sleep and was let off when they slowed down out front about day-light. He'd shoot ducks all day and be home to fiddle at night! That's the kind of a hunter he was. A droll, gruff old Bismarck type, with an exterior and expression like the giant's who made Jack-in-the-Beanstalk break all existing records for pole sliding. But skin-under no kind-

lier soul ever lived. He belonged to all the hunting and
fishing clubs pretty much, built their boats and blinds
and lockers and never did a bad job in his life. No one
could match his scroll saw work and when it came to
what we hunters of today call "kinks," I believe the
Professor had forgotten more of them than our mod-
erns will ever learn. The Professor! Salute!

Mister Tim O'Dare was a saloonkeeper and not
ashamed of it. Nor was any one of our people I ever
heard of ashamed of him or his business. What is there
to be ashamed of in a Christian gentleman and a very
gallant old Confederate soldier, or a Yankee, either,
for that matter? He said his prayers every night I ever
saw him go to bed in the house or out under the stars,
and the good Lord knows he sold only the finest old
whiskies and ales and porters he could import. He
never sold a "mixed drink" or sold to a minor or
"drunk!" He never sold to a woman or allowed one to
enter his place. He never "kept open" on Sunday and
he "closed up" promptly at ten o'clock every night.
And he never knowingly sold any one man more than
three drinks, said he "didn't belave in ut!" When pro-
hibition first came Mister Tim never questioned the
mandate. " 'Tis the Law," said he. He shut up shop—
quit cold—retired to his farm; gave away what was
left of his liquor stock to "auld fri'nds," and that was
the end of it. He had long since amassed a fortune and

editors had written citations of him as a model in his "line!" Naturally, in his early times I've heard that Mister Tim never dodged even the remote chance or prospect of any physical encounter; he must have been what they term nowadays a "fightin' fool."

My first visit to Mister Tim's place is as vivid a memory as the Professor's theatre. Dad had been "summonsed" to the old courthouse as a witness in a big lawsuit—the courthouse was a block or so north of Mister Tim's, where the forlorn "For Rent" sign is now. Dad was on the stand a long time, and two of the lawyers had fines clapped on them for fighting in court, if you call fighting hurling law books at each other at three paces and missing. It was custom in those days for lawyers with or without an excuse or case, to "recess" in Mister Tim's bar for a snort of liquor or ice cold beer, and a snack of his celebrated free lunch. Highest minds of the law and mighty minds of finance got down onto a common level of the love of good liquor in Tim's domain. There were only two or three marble-topped tables where three-drink-limit men with afternoon cases had the call on sitting privileges. Other folks drammed standing up—going back and forth from where an old darky named Shorty presided over the lunch. Of a Monday, for instance, Shorty served barbecued lamb; on Tuesday roast pork ham; Wednesday, prime rib roast, and Thursday mayhap a

Brunswick stew — everything smothered in gravy that is today practically a lost art — Shorty's dead. There was a huge white hickory basket full of sweet, crispy homemade bread, and hot mustard that got up your nose if you took too much, and young onions and a raft of cheeses to sniff over. Shorty had to stand on an upended wash tub to get right-o'-way, and what he called "purchase" with his long, razor-sharp carving knife. Nobody was ashamed of an appetite or capacity in those days, and Mister Tim didn't give a rap how much anyone got away with. There was considerable ceremony attached to Shorty's turning out a feed. First he'd smile and bow and then get under way by drenching a double palm of that home-made bread with gravy and strewing it with particles of lingering outside crispies. Then he'd lay on it a man's size slice of whatever meat he had for the day and respectfully ask your own selection as to a slab of mustard or ladle of overpowering horse-radish. The partaker by that time was usually in the most advanced stage of appetite and ready with a nickel or dime that never slid out of Shorty's greasy palm. And by the time you'd got back alongside the polished mahogany, Mister Tim or one of the helpers had whisked a bell-mouthed schooner of amber or dark brew afront of you, deftly combed off its beard of froth and left you alone with the joy of a combination of food and drink hard to beat.

Do you wonder that I was greatly taken with the place, notably with Shorty's end of it after Dad had a sandwich fixed for me? Mister Tim's bar flashed multi-colored reflections from enormous mirrors, gay bottles with lemons and oranges and bunches of purple grapes — the old chap had an eye for color! Paintings of crack racehorses and winning field dogs adorned the walls and over the center of the bar was a huge picture of the late John L. Sullivan, depicting him in the buff and set for action. Along the north wall of the room, and lit by a basin of reflectors, hung a gigantic and well-executed oil painting — a boulder-strewn cascade in the foreground and overhung pools beyond. On a mossy bank reclined a fisherman, fly rod aslant of him and a goodly mess of hefty trout spilling from an over-turned creel. You could look at the strong-chinned, dark-haired, roughly clad and rightly shod youth of the picture and then glance at Mister Tim and tell it for an oil memory of his Irish boyhood. "Divil a bit," I've heard him say to Mister Arthur and Dad, who thought no more of taking me into Mister Tim's place than letting their bird dogs come along, "woold I mind bein' back there this minit, Miles, along o' th' bruuke wid a bit o' cheese in me pockut an' me poipe — an' what'll yez be havin', fri'nd?" — as some long-coated lawyer bellied his way to the bar. And having served him, Mister Tim would come back and fall to talking

[47]

guns and dogs and hunting and ducks! That was thirty years ago or better and much of that talk has stood me in good stead ever since.

The Professor and Mister Tim came to the Chickasaw Bluffs long, long before there was even a cloud on the civil horizon or a rift in the sky of Secession. I've heard them tell of shooting quail and ducks where some of our largest factories and buildings stand to-day! When the war "broke out" they enlisted in the same company and "fit thru" together. They came home and chose home sites in the same end of town. The Professor raised a big family of tall sons and Mister Tim just one stocky lad, who went away with his mother later on and left Mister Tim's sister, Miss Brigid, to mother and look after him. His walled-in, twenty-acre farm lay in the outer outskirts of the city then — a tiny, old-fashioned conglomerate cottage effect squatting amid a grove of magnificent oaks. There were hay fields and barns and orchards of luscious peaches and sappy, snappy apples. And such big fruit!

I doubt if two more ostensibly bitter enemies ever lived than Mister Tim and the Professor. The former clumped downtown of a morning and sought out the Professor in his loafing place in the apothecary's office. Then, to quote him, he "preceeded t' cuss out th' dommed auld Dutchman!" They cussed each other out every day on general principles or issues of the press. They fussed all the way home again. They agreed on anything opposite. Each one's equipment for duck shooting or fishing outclassed the other's to hear him tell it. German guns outshot all other guns except Irish-made weapons — even Mister Tim went to the defense of English gun-building. If the Professor appeared with some novel and costly appliance, Mister Tim at once sent abroad for something to outdo it. Their club lockers were in opposite ends of the room— they argued and bickered back and forth — it was a stream of "Bosh — Tim — bosh" and "Nonsense — Dutchy — nonsense." They sniggered and writhed and insulted each other in the euchre game. And yet, in all the years I knew them, did I ever see or hear of one's going hunting or fishing without the other! Once in a while they were separated, but such trips were never a success. "If I'd 'a had Tim along" or "If thot dommed Dutchman had been with me"— that was the alibi. Nor did I ever fail to see them forget to kneel by their respective old-fashioned walnut beds and bow their white heads in earnest prayer. The turned-down bedtime lamp would flicker out and then you'd hear "Goo' night, Dutchy," and "Night, Irish," growled across the gloom.

If Irish drew a good blind and Dutchy a poor prospect for the day's duck shooting, they might leave the clubhouse nagging at each other and pull out in opposite directions, but before long you'd hear their two guns at work in Mister Tim's neighborhood. They fought, bled and never settled the question of supremacy with the shotgun. They disputed the bag and its division and went home wrangling — but inevitably together! They are neighbors yet, out in the cemetery.

Better than twenty years ago I poled my tiny duck boat one glorious November morning to the shallows in the far south end of old Beaver Dam Lake. Thence I dragged it across mud flats and swamp stumps to shelter in a cluster of button willows and tulles. Mallards were swinging in off the main lake and across it, a good half mile away; another club member had moved in and began popping away on a fine flight. I could plainly see the birds decoy; hear his live stools open up in a chorus of deceitful welcome and see a bird or so go tumbling long before the reports of his gun came across on the breeze. At length a fine green-headed mallard sailed high past me and, ignoring my frantic invitation to "light," set his wings to a magnificent glide to my unknown neighbor's trap. Two jets of white squirted from the hide. I saw the bird stagger, fall away a bit and then, recovering, sail directly toward me, with that stiff, telltale, wobbly movement indicative of a fatal body shot and quick collapse. Just outside my decoys he gave up the battle, and plunged into the loblolly, dead as a hammer. So, being close to my own "limit" of ducks, I picked it up and, paddling across the lake, tossed the drake to the occupant of the blind — Mister Tim. He thanked me with a courteous sincerity that amply repaid a stripling — as if youth minded anyway! That evening, in the clubhouse, he thanked me again. After that season I went away to college and saw but little of the two old gentlemen for several years. We'll skip that period and discover me with a tiny business and office of my own; a "grown-up" membership in Beaver Dam — and a meeting of the club set for an October afternoon. Into my office came Mister Tim, grizzled, rough, rugged in his working-man's exterior that gave no hint of his substantial means. He spread before me a great sheaf of policies covering his large real estate holdings and told me to "look after them for him." The amount made me gasp and when I tried to thank him in a profuse, bewildered sort of fashion, he looked at me with a quizzical grin and squint of shrewd Irish blue eyes boring at me along the stem of his corn-cob pipe, and said, "D'yez mind, yoong mon, that duuke — that mallid duuke — yez paddled acroose th' lake an' gi' t' me that arfternoon long years ago — d' yez mind it noo?" I said, rather faintly, that I thought I remembered it. "That's why, thin'," he continued, pointing to the papers, "whin yez did that for me, I sez t' myself, I sez, 'Tim,' I sez, 'there's a hones' yoongling done an' ould man a sportin' tourn an' I'll try t' do th' same b' him soome day.' Noo — naaar — don' be thankin' me no more, lad. G'wan an' write thim oop, but noo put on yez hat an' coom wid me an' vote agi'n thot dommed Dutchman at th' meetin'. Would yez b'lave it, he's fixin' t' outvote me!" Good luck and good-bye, old staunch heart!

Barring the love and affection of real mankind for its ilk of manhood, there is no love theme to this little story. Since that meeting of the club in October of that year, a wealth of "water has run under the bridge." The Professor and Mister Tim are both past the four-score mark — and I — well, never mind about me. But still they go "a-hunting." And then, suddenly, Miss Brigid, Mister Tim's sister, died. I'd paid him a visit scarce a week before — just dropped in on the gentleman. He came up from the hayfield to meet me. Pushing a laden wheelbarrow pulled ridges into his still heavily corded arms; sweat trickled down upon a full chest open to any lingering breeze. What a speci-men for past mid-eighty! Another week, which put upon him the blight and ordeal of Miss Brigid's pass-ing, and I looked upon a weak, stricken old man! Two of "us boys" went to cheer him up — to talk fishing and plan a trip down to the club with him and the Pro-fessor for guests of honor. We found him slouched in an old rocker, staring straight ahead — wretchedly

feeble. We tried our best, but it was dismal failure —
cruelly impossible. He had tongue only for Miss Brigid
— her love for him, her care of him and the void he
faced without her. " 'Twill be little hoonting I'll be
a-doin' noo," he murmured; "little hoonting. You lads
take what's mine an' kape it. D'yez mind thim waders
in me locker — thim's yures — an' th' ould Greener
goon — there's no wan prizes it like you — take it,
lad! An' give Horace t' other goon — th' artymatic—
he's a good naygur; an' giv' 'im th' lambwool under-
wear I brung from th' ould country — an' you kape
thim decoys." We cried out to him to stop — that he'd
live to shoot many another duck, that he'd live to be
so ancient they'd have to blow him in at Judgment Day
— but it all fell upon deaf ears and almost unseeing
eyes. So we left him, crouched, mooning in the shaky
rocker with a sheaf of sunlight sifting about him
through a crack in the umbrage of a giant oak. Three
mornings later his old darky, Lazrus, couldn't wake
him, nor could the doctor Lazrus ran wildly for —
Mister Tim had "racked up." There being only an odd
grandchild or so, some of "us boys" went out and sat
up with Mister Tim, in his tiny parlor crowded with
stuffed ducks and fish and sea shells and a collection of
pistols and dirks. There was a bright-eyed canary, too,
that Mister Tim set a lot of store by. He'd stand at the
cage and carry on a confab which the pert inmate

seemed to really understand, and never passed through the parlor without handing in a bit of lettuce or a sprig of seed or a saucer of water.

The Professor came over that night, red-eyed, solemn and unbending in his dumb grief. When it got late we tried to make him go home, but the harder we wheedled the more stubbornly he refused. He finally agreed, though, to take off his long Sunday coat and stiff choker collar and sit outside in a "lay-back" chair — where it was cool, and we hoped he'd fall asleep. He did nap occasionally, and, coming out of one, would walk over to the casket and look down intently into the calm, almost smiling face of his comrade.

A suspicion of summer dawn drifted across my face. A heightening blush and a sweet breath of fruity dew breathing past the curtains. And with it, songsters of the free outside and Mister Tim's pet of the gilded cage awoke. Their chorus trilled and thrilled, met and mingled above the bier of their protector and friend — it was just the music Mister Tim would have liked best for his "leaving out." I have stood at attention and felt my pulse quicken to the thunder and roll of burial anthems — dead marches and the sonorous tribute of band and organ — but nothing as sweet and tender and peaceful as the farewell of those songsters to Mister Tim. A shadow fell across the kitchen doorway and there stood the Professor with the same look in his tired red eyes that Mister Tim carried that afternoon he cried for Miss Brigid. The Professor had put on his long coat and stiff collar — he was set for the ordeal of the crossroads. Slowly he retraced his paths of the night that led to the side of his Pal, and stood smiling wistfully upon him.

"Professor," said I, "run along home now — there's nothing you can do until ten o'clock. I'll have Lazrus drip you some coffee and rake up a snack — you'll feel better — and then you run along over home."

The Comrade drew himself to his full height, his lips suddenly quivering in a vain effort at control, his bosom rose and fell in a futile effort to stifle the storm of sobs that sent a gust of tears scalding down upon his old puff tie and its companion Confederate button that matched the one in Mister Tim's lapel. 'Twas a bursting of the dam, the rush of affectionate, pent-up waters held in the reservoir of life.

"Go — go — home?" he queried, wiping his eyes and facing me down with a look that brooked no denial of purpose. "Go home and leaf' Tim? No-no-NO! Dese many yeahs Tim und I haf been togedder — I — I — go vid Tim — chus so far — es I can!"

BOB WHITE BLUE! BOB WHITE GRAY!

Evelyn's response was characteristic. "Entirely all right and welcome to include the Colonel. The right hand of fellowship to his Yankee breeding. If he's a good shot (and he must be or you wouldn't be playing around with him) and don't mind "cawn toddies," okay to his pass-port. Plenty of birds and my dogs in such high fettle I'd better be knocking on wood. I'll meet you in town. It'll be New Year's eve so we'll simply have to stay awhile for the Court House ball. Hal will put us up for dinner at the old home place. If the road is as bad as I suspect it will be, we'll load the plunder into Jack's wagon and drive on out to Brick House."

So, in abundant glow of anticipation that brooked no dwindling of enthusiasm, Hal and I and the Colonel from "Vermawnt" came to Brick House to gun Bob White with Evelyn. Perhaps I ought to say "came back," for to Hal and me it is almost "home." True to Ev's prediction there had been heavy rains. Our trek to the "old home place" led through stately old Aberdeen. Past the huge courthouse, crumbly with its struggle against the years; reminiscent of impassioned oratory and bitter but courtly legal battles. At intervals, we glimpsed through spacious boundaries of wintry cedar hedges, towering, leafless oaks. And resting amid winding rose walks and arborous gardens, old fashioned homes of singular and comforting beauty. Some with their broad porches and superb lines of colonial panelling drooping into an almost sagging dilapidation of Civil War impoverishment. Others bespeaking an eloquent survival of defiance of time.

I am firm in the belief that nowhere on earth is the real pleasure of friendship and Christmas value so well preserved or deeply cognizant of its own tender ties as at the Yuletide ball in an old aristocratic southern community. These festive gatherings are held each year, just as were predecessors of like step and fancy, in either the town-hall or court-house. In our particular happy instance the assembly room of the municipal building, waxed as to floor and festooned with crimson berried holly and inviting mistletoe past any semblance to the austere forum of political and legal strife, was thronged with gay couples. The music, changed only through the encroachment of hitherday step and tune, never really in personnel of players or true substance of melody, "swayed valiant summons to the dance."

From beyond home circles came guests from smaller towns and regional cities. Beautiful visiting misses armed with charming darts aimed directly at unshrinking home stalwarts! College lads in newly acquired dignity, and amazingly adept in the latest flights and fancies of Terpsichore. Everywhere one encountered well-set-up men and lovely girls, radiant together in a warmth of genuine and cordial reunion and jovial familiarity of life-long association. In some cases appeared unmistakably perceptible symptoms of far deeper interest.

Along the high windowed walls, beneath portraits of distinguished legal kin and departed but not forgotten courtiers of the bench or bar, sat grave old gentlemen whose dress suits, for the most part, bespoke a vintage of remote years, and gave off, upon the occasion of an affectionate slap upon the shoulder a subtle, yet nevertheless convincing odor of camphor. Beside them sat sweet little silver-haired ladies, very, very dear to the hearts of all concerned. These gravely smiling old gentlemen in their camphorated tails and their little old ladies in queenly silks, had danced here in their own bright long agos — just as their sons and daughters and grandchildren were doing now. It was good to realize, too, that yonder, come all the way home for the holidays sat President J., of the great B. & L. system; that sitting proudly beside one of the

dear old sweet ladies, in place of his father, the Colonel — was Doctor E., famous surgeon the world over.
The beaux and belles were there to uphold the right of
modernity; those who had gone forth and returned
laden with success were present because to them, this,
with all its loved memories was home. There were no
harsh words or uncomely thoughts for those who had
fared away so bravely only to return rebuffed and
down-hearted. For them, as for everyone, the level
eye of kindliness and a hand of heart-meant good
cheer. There was brave, sad fortitude and greening
memory for those who could never return. Hands
sometimes clasp hands at these dances where the
garden of years had grown rank with weeds of bitter-
ness and cold restraint. Land suits and petty fallings-
out of the neighborhood are perchance settled out of
court across the punch bowl; indictments of love
argued and dismissed. The blood and bone and sinew
of a clan come together in a blending of "peace on
earth, good will toward men" at the Christmas dance
in their Old Home Town.

We have lent ear to good music and foot to the
dance. Now for the long, long road to Brick House.
Thank goodness for an honest "hack" with spring
seat and mettlesome "hay-burners." I'm sick of gaso-
line and upholstered leather on shooting trips. "Watch
that off-mule, Jack, he's fixing to load us all skyward."

Coat collars up and a jolt off into the dark. Now to navigate through and out of town in the mule manner and like it.

They built the brick house, so Aunt Dora's crone of a Black Mammy told me in her cabin one night years ago, "long 'bout som'time befo' ol' Cunn'l hisse'f clamb up on he big white hawss an' rid off t' fight wid d' Mexicums!" In so definitely affirming this relevantly important reminiscence, Granny Captola inhaled three sucky draws upon the sparky dregs of her usually over-stuffed corn-cob pipe and solemnly knotholed two highly accurate sluicings of "ham gravy dip" into the sputtery ashes of her cavernous chimney hollow. She could almost remember, she said, "seein' de stars fall, an' know'd all 'bout how ol' Satan riz up same as saleratus raises in de biscuits an' shuk all de lan' t'well h'it reel an rock an' de ground sunk an' de big ribber runned back'uds!" You figure it out, if you've a mind to, how long ago that cosmic upheaval took place.

They called it the Brick House then, and the name has stuck right down to this day. "They" means a pitiful remnant such as Granny Captola herself, for example, and a few remote others bedded about in hutches and cross-roads burying grounds, mostly with one or both feet in the grave. And pretty much all the rest are descendants of those who "toted" and sawed

and broad-axed to help clear it. Brick House is citadel
and community center! How naturally, hopefully and
sometimes with almost wistful respect the black folks
look to it for advice and aid. Nor rarely in vain — God
be praised! To its front door for solution of those
perplexing things they know they must do, but with
castdown eyes to its back door for absolution from those
things they know they ought not to have done.

Go a long piece off across Big Sandy bottoms, where
the "humpty-dumpty" road to town tumbles into a
deep, shady gash that brings teams or automobiles out
panting and puffing high above the Great Marsh and
from there you first glimpse Brick House, looming
castle-like on its bench at the shoulder of McClellan's
Grove. Off to the northeast fifteen or twenty miles is
where for many and many a year, over much the same
lovely quail country of swale, thicket and wastrel gully
land as surrounds Brick House, field trial contenders
have matched stride and sagacity for national hunting
supremacy of the upland. And not so very far to the
southeast, the upper reaches of another famous old
field trial course peters out on the slope of Persimmon
Ridge. It, too, knew the stifled ambitions, the joyous
heart throbs and questings of a race of upstanding
pioneer sportsmen and brainy, wide-going, iron-lunged
bird dogs. It is a land of engaging and cordial hospi-
talities fully in keeping with its legends of largess. It

is a land of innate sporting lore handed down from father to son, of fox hound strains and blue blood in setters and pointers. But above and best of all, it is a land of unabashed, level-eyed yeomanry, of frugality and toil well repaid in nourishing and self-respecting yield!

Well, then, you rattle and bump and squeak across one after another of Big Sandy's runs, spoored with bird and rabbit and "varmint" paddings; drag gradually uphill again for a couple of country miles, and pop out all of a sudden right in front of Brick House! There you are! A formal front yard, palisaded with hand-drawn white oak staves; a limpety-crackety gate and a shrub and flower-bordered walk of curiously cobbled squares. An alleyway, overhung by stately oaks and fringed sweepingly with interliners of gnome-like, berried cedars. In summer time long bladed grasses are sacheted with locust and honey-suckle crumblings, and flirty southwinds strew the lawn with muslin mull from dogwood and peach orchard. The lovable homestead is a babel of chortling bird life. Nests are woven or swung aloft in a charming profusion of unvigilant domesticity. From fields and woods lot come the mingled low-noted plaint and quavering "Cheerio" of dove and bob white. But in winter, layer upon layer of leafy mold carpets, jonquil and hyacinth. Tender bulbs and cuttings are hooded in loam for their long, warm sleep. And Brick House, shorn of its joyous camaraderie of song and cloying sweetness, bares its seamed, weather-wrought old face to the challenge of storms and stresses it has never feared.

Clump into its austere but welcoming center hall! Never mind the mud on your boots and leave the dogs be! "Here with the bootjack — you with the poached-egg eyes — do some yanking and scraping or find yourself in the middle of a tough something!" Pile your bird hunter's plunder in Captain Ev's bedroom — over yonder — it used to be the parlor, when crinoline waltzed to the "Mocking Bird!" Now look about you.

Rare old furniture everywhere and more of it sheathed in storage in the vast attic. Thump those paneled doors and toe those hewn floor boards — wide as your forearm is long. What massive sills and beams, and such plaster. Not a sag or a crack! Here and there, though, you'll notice bogs of brick and mortar gouged from side walls, and some of the windows have splintery holes drilled through the panes and ugly slug cavities in the shutters. Aunt Dora grinningly tells "outside folks:" "Dem wuz done du'in war times, yaas suh — when us fit wid d' Yankees — ol' Cap'n ain' nuvvr 'lowed nobody t' put in no new glass — says he want 'em t' stay jes' lak dey wuz made — an' ef' nobody don't lak de wind whistlin' thu dem bullet holes —

den dey kin' jes' buil' up de fiah an' git closer to h'it." And Aunt Dora dies off in a gale of suppressed merriment that agitates each and every one of her amplifications!

Then, if you like, come along and we'll ramble down around the moss roofed, saggy old barn, with its blended odors of oat crunchings, currycombings and sweaty leather. What a litter of trace chains, mule collars, plow points, axle grease and rusty junk! Grunty porkers nose about and soft-eyed Moo-Cows moo, turn bovine scrutiny after us.

Lacings of red pepper strings and pottle gourds, bundles of warping fish canes, bow-legged urchins and huge iron wash pots are jumbled about the "Quarters." And the same oft-tolling plantation bell, tottery on its aged stilts, still "rings in and rings out," just as it began calling along about the time Granny Captola claims she almost saw the stars fall!

Brick House smiles a rare and all-embracing welcome the full width of its classic facings. It seems to say: "Come along with you, young folks — I've minded generations of you through sunshine and shadow — all of us Old Timers have — light down and hitch, for fox hunters and bird shooters — I know every one of you — sweethearts and wives and good old dogs and jumpers — aye — and your Daddies and Gran' Daddies, too — hurry up — come on in he'ah —

I miss you and I'm getting along — I'm yo' *home!*"

So, look affectionately if not reverently upon Brick House. Go close to it. Feel of its oddly shaped, time-dulled red bricks patted into shape and burned by slave hands that were such in loyalty only. Do this as I am not ashamed to confess having done, with a comforting sense of pride in heritage.

And, if I am not very much mistaken and disappointed, something will whisper to you as it did to me: "All such stalwart and noble homes, faithful tenantry and toilsome lands about them must endure as most representative and worthy in the preservation of American ideals — swear to it — deep down in your hearts — that all they have stood for shall never stand for contamination." Whether they drowse in the land of cotton, beaten biscuits and beautiful women, or cling, by the sign of the sacred codfish and sap of the maple sugar bucket, to the rock-ribbed true blue hills of Old New England!

Brick House at last, though the hour is midnight. Wood fires snapping. Welcoming lamp light. Ministering black hands. Innumerable silhouettes in reserve. Evelyn speaking — "You bed in that corner, Colonel — yonder for you all, Buck and Hal — and I'll bunk in this corner (four "four posters" in one chamber, think of it) — shake a leg, Will, quick with the sugar and water — you're slipping."

Jack bustles in, doubling from hostler to bus boy — the fastest passer of hot biscuits on earth. A timid emissary from Aunt Dora's culinary domain: "a l'il bite t'eat raidy." A vast dining room; cheerful hearth spotted with plates warming — great brand of service Jack puts out. Lofty china closets and wainscoted silver vaults. Considerable clatteration from the kitchen. Aunt Dora's strident voice demanding less fuss and inviting several sitters-below-the-salt, to "git outa he'ah now — git on outa he'ah I says — naw — I ain' gwin' giv' you much ez er mouf'ful — git on out fo' I busts you side de haid wid dis skillet."

Did I say a "snack?" Fluffy omelet, Sally Lunn, country butter, native honey. "Which do you crave, Colonel?" asks Ev, spooning discerningly into the smoky eruption of a pot pie's dome — "chicken bosom, rabbit thigh, spare parts, or just considerable of ev'ything?" The Colonel requisitions full company rations. Jack, meanwhile, stages a whirlwind campaign, reporting to the kitchen that "Mista Nash had done et a lot befo' hit seem lak his appetite done really come to him." Deaf to his entreaties, we stagger to the east room profoundly burthened.

Enter Gus. For all the world a Weller senior, in low chocolate. Tightish pantaloons tucked into gaitered bootees, sleek embonpoint sheltered in a sheep-lined surtout and a gay scarf at his throat to polish off effects sartorial. He has prodded his favorite mule a long way for this important conference and its invariably delectable aftermath! An influential and faithful henchman, Gus! Owner of fat kine, full barn, an unmortgaged tilling and lengthy stair-stepping of cotton-pickin' chilluns. No mean hand at repartee, Gus! The examination gets under way —

"You been well, Gus?"

"Well, — that is — er — I bin' tol'able — thanke, suh, Cap'n."

"No chest pains, chilblains, falling arches or flaming youth?" Gus registers searching personal diagnosis and denies any symptoms relative to this four out of five perspective.

"Your mule all right, too, Gus?"

"Yaas, suh, him an' me 'bout alike."

Will Joy, grinning Master of the Kennel, is next in line and steps one pace forward! Will admits to me later that "he wouldn' swap jobs wid nobody — I got de bes' Boss Man in de whole worl' — if I dooes wrong an' he fiah me — which lak he'll sho' do, too — I gwi' crawl back abeggin' on my han's an' knees — when Cap'n says, 'DO DIS'— I know he means — 'DO DIS'— an' das de way hits gwi' git dooed!"

A sound philosophy and far sighted policy, William! Jack and Aunt Dora, their dishes done, are now standing in the delegation.

"What dogs do we take tomorrow, Will?"

"Us better take de Ol' Man — Joe — an' maybe Nellie — an' Seymour — an' sho'ly les' us take da' puppy o' mine, da Jim dawg — Cap'n, he gwi be a sho' nuff dawg. You all gwi' walk or ride — Cap'n?"

"We'll walk tomorrow — be here at 8 o'clock sharp, Will." Will becomes a file closer. Gus recaptures the spotlight. The Captain's tone becomes grave. "Gus, how is the Coaster?" At mention of the Coaster the entire group is mantled in concern. Gus straightens and "a-h-e-m-m-s" throatily, several times.

"He dooes ve'y well, Cap'n — leas' ways he wuz so doin' de las time I had bizness wid 'im!"

"His choir been practicin' regularly an' improving right along?"

"Yaas, suh, Cap'n, dey dooes putty well now, suh, considerin' — "

"Considerin' what?"

"Well, suh-uh-uh considerin' — considerin' — de consideration he bin able to giv' 'em — y' know, Cap'n, deys mos' done bin twins com' t'ide Coaster's house!" Gus beams! Chorus of "Sho' is bin!" from the ensemble.

"Who sings soprano now?" Deep meditation. Aunt Dora comes to the rescue. "Cap'n, de reg'lar s'prano done bin had er turble col' — misery all up in his ches' — bin had de doctor wid 'im — nuther young nigger

[69]

bin spellin' him in de choir — but he 'bout all right again now — de herb practor bin lately radicatin' him wid possum grease salve."

"Suppose you can persuade the Coaster to bring his choir over tomorrow night and sing for the Colonel — you and Will and Jack are elders in the Household of the Loyal Order, ain't you?" Thus severally and individually identified as accomplices to prominence, a special whispered Board Meeting is held, the caucus rendering a pronouncement committing the Coaster's choir sight unseen and song unsung. There being apparently no further business to come before the meeting, "excusin'" as Aunt Dora would say, the most important matter of all — the company fidgets. Sensing this, Captain relieves the situation by dispensing a liberal nightcap. Acknowledgment of hearty wishes for joint safekeeping throughout the night — and we are alone.

Colonel and Captain are soon hard at it again — in France! Under cover of a barrage of apparently desultory but effective minor preparations, Ye Chronicler, betaking himself to a deep and downy billet, lies listening — snatches of trench talk fend off raids of overmastering drowsiness — "Do you remember — uuuummm — around by Nantillois — that bridge head at Bethencourt — direct fire — hell, wasn't it — Verdun — we went over on the fourteenth — it was up by *Chemin des Dames* — coal scuttles — took cover like rabbits — shrapnel — more blood and guts than you ever saw — Heinies — Frogs — rain — barbed wire — more rain — guns oriented — kilometers — cognac — Paris — wine — the damned M. P.'s!''

A black shape at my bedside — Jack, with a cheery "Good mawnin', Boss," and an aromatic cedar bucket from which he ladles an eye-opener of icy cistern water. He sets a dazzling pace at breakfast — broiled pork steaks with creamy gravy, matched sets of eggs and biscuits and joyful Java! Dogs barking outside and Will Joy bows in, accoutred for the chase. "Why the rabbit sack, Will?" "Well, suh, you knows I allus did favor *them* boys!"

Mr. Porter rides up to acknowledge introductions and pass salutations. Mr. Porter is a gentleman of some seventy-odd years of intimate contact with the policies and "grapevines" of the county. The captain's carryings-on are Mr. Porter's for delivery, and in such course he has an M.A. degree. He promptly suspects and challenges the Colonel's being a "Vermawnter." Judgment therefore is suspended until further facts are developed. We assemble outside. A gray morning — squalls lulled, but a sullen, leaden jumble on the horizon, liable to start anything. But the ground is in great shape for dog work! Mr. Porter stands to horse, throwing a deft leg over his skittish pinto colt. We branch off at the lane bars — "you boys be sho' now an' stop off by my house for a snack aroun' about noon time," he admonishes. A parting shot from the young Captain — "don't let that pin ear sling you off, Mr. Porter," elicits a curled lip from the old gentleman — "'i'Gad if he does it'll be th' fust one evuh done it!'"

The dogs have scattered to work. We round off onto a high point, magnificent vistas of quail country rolling to the skyline through open piney clumps. Flashing spots off across the valley — the dogs! On a distant hillside Will Joy wig-wags. "Joe's gone that way," codes Ev, and we swing to the southeast. You'll doubt what I'm telling you now about Joe, a great rangy, black and white ticked pointer of the old school — a throwback to days of real bone and sinew and minds, twelve year old Joe! One of those really magnificent bird-finders of all time — unsung, perhaps, but not unhonored! His original blinding speed has slackened a trifle, but not his space-devouring lope, uncanny nose and supreme bird sense. Foot-hunting behind Joe is a cross-country chase with Will Joy as liaison officer. More wig-wagging from Will — Joe has located his first bevy!

By the time we get up, the three setters are backing here and there on the outskirts of a briar-bordered plum thicket with puppy Jim watching Will Joy for orders.

The Colonel circles a devious route toward where Will points out Joe, up ahead and a taut symbol of real pointer form. We edge in a trifle. The Colonel's new 20-gauge is going up for its baptism of fire. The thicket explodes and takes wing — a single whisks my way and is tumbled. "What about the gun? How'd the Owen go?" "Oh, fine," he stammers with delighted excitement. "Think I made a double!"

This prove to be the case, and never minding singles, we climb the ravine. Will Joy is already far ahead on the route — Joe has cast that way and can be seen when we reach the crest — a speck of blurred white lashing a hillside. An hour later, with several finds behind us, we are in the deep woods. Only puppy Jim has done a solo stunt on birds to keep pace with the Old Master; but it was a staunch reward for industry, and Will's pride knows no bounds. A shout from Will, for Joe is at it again up there in the open woods. But nothing happens when we close in. Something wrong here! No telling how long he's been standing there — they've run off — give him a little time — get on, Old Head! The other dogs back trail, cold trail, and "some tall inquestin'," as Will puts it, goes forward. But the Old Master, cutting a slashing half circle, suddenly whips to the right, high headed — no foolishness with him! He's nailed them this time. "Cock your musket, Colonel, we'll defend the Manor House with our lives!"

"Zooks," he mutters, when the uproar has subsided
— "if only the little beggars wouldn't fluster the living daylights out of me when they beat it," — Will
Joy is pointing on ahead — "Dey drapped 'long side
da' I'll dreen." The dogs had three singles spotted but
we passed them up and six more that we flushed, watching the spat-throated cocks and mottled hens whip
swirling back to wood's haven for another season.
"Good luck to you, you gallant little rascals!" The
dogs have all disappeared and we separate, searching
for a bevy point. A brooding, gray stillness pressing
about, with a few wisping crumbs of snow — surely it
won't last. But suddenly big, wet flakes come tumbling,
faster and faster. "Head for Mr. Porter's across the
hollow yonder," calls Ev through the blizzard.

We put our best feet forward — the downfall is beginning to stick, and the dogs are worried — even
old Joe comes in. Just before we angle uphill he suddenly wheels to one side and points into a fallen tree
top. We catch a glimpse of hovering birds afoot —
and then they are away through the brush, and the
Colonel being handy scores a right barrel. "Where my
experience as an old New England pah'tridge shooter
stood me in good stead," he explains. Mr. Porter's comfortable home dispenses dyed-in-the-wool good cheer.
Takes women folks to make matters just right. Jack
meets us with the wagon. "Take Joe home," instructs

Ev, "give him a possum salve rub and bed him down soft. Fetch back Dan and Ned. If it clears we'll go on; if it doesn't we'll make a red day for the rabbits — how about it, Mr. Porter?" Mr. Porter, field trial impresario emeritus, sniffs disdainfully — "like a passel o' boys — runnin' rabbits in th' snow — I might go 'long tho'!"

Too bounteous a board, Mr. Porter's, for an impending hard afternoon of it. "If you see me bog down on some low ground," mouths the Colonel, shifting gears in a wedge of meringued sweet potato pie, "leave me, I entreat thee, I'll only be putting on my chains and going into second." The Mason and Dixon's line issue is touched upon lightly but none-the-less positively, Mr. Porter, as host, assuming a most chivalrous bearing. "I ain't sayin' it o' cose, 'caus you come from V'mont, Colonel, but back in '82, I think it wuz — two Yank — er — two No'then boys settled in he'ahbouts, an' when 'lection time rolled 'round, two-three o' th' Vig'lance committee come t' me an' say — s'i' — 'Them fellers ain't fixin t' try t' vote, is they?' — right then an' there s'i — 'right is right — if you all votes — they votes — whut good is it goin' t' do them, nohow'!" The Colonel, not to be outdone in any exchange of generosities, pays high tribute to the fighting qualities of some Southern boys with whom he soldiered. "Fight?" avers Mr. Porter grumblingly;

[75]

"Fight? — o' cose' th' Hell they'll fight!"

But time has flown, brilliant sunshine has cut away the storm and Jack is on hand with a relay of fresh dogs. We bid goodbye to Mr. Porter and strike off east through the rapidly disappearing slush. "Fourteen bevies this forenoon," counts up Ev; "twelve of them for Joe." Dan, a hard-going young setter, proves the afternoon's hero. What a ramble we take, into territory that even Ev hasn't penetrated all season, clear around the headwaters of the Great Marsh, picking a cautious, mucky way across an arm of it trying to locate some crafty singles.

"Pretty much anything in here you want'" remarks Hal, "duck, woodcock, snipe." We find the largest of six bevies just before we climb the backbone of a ridge that slopes from Brick House and almost divides the Marsh. Brick House again — bulking huge against a serried sunset of plum and gold. Frost in the offing, cows plodding up from the pasture, a darky chunking clods and yodelling. Jack is the mainstay from then on — Jack with his fires going, hot water and towels and cold water and sugar; Jack with the slippers and easy chairs. Jack hot footing it about another table laden to nourish the inner man — good, faithful Jack!

We retire for coffee, and preparations for the Coaster's visit go forward. Rumbling wagons unload a considerable gathering, with whispered doings-about for the ceremony. We are finally summoned to the west room. Two long, high-backed pews have been arranged before the fireplace. We are introduced and given seats to the rear. The Coaster stands aloof, a tall, solemn personage of almost monastic mien, a Savonarola in *cafe au lait!* He holds a glistening peeled hickory baton. His choristers arrange themselves along the pews. Jack, it develops, handles basso profundo. Aunt Dora, Will and sundry other pot-wallopers are grouped as congregation to the service. The Coaster raises an impressive arm. Silence. Pointed fire darts lick high into pilastered mouldings; the chamber is in half darkness.

"We'll firs' reques' Brother Lovingood t' lead us in prayer." A grizzled and heavy-lidded Elder rises and in all reverence speaks a worthy plea for souls such as ours — God forbid that I speak in levity here in the presence of an engaging and simple strength of Faith — "LORD our CHRIST," he entreats, his countenance alight with zeal and his sonorous exhortation deepening into fervid texture, "look down upon us we beseech THEE as strivin' in ouh 'umble way t' show 'preciation o' THY power an' GLORY — mek us thankful O!LORD that all YO' CHILLUN'S voices be raised in THY glo'fication an' that YOU may rejoice, too, O! LORD that we can have come with us into THY PRESENCE this evenin' — the hearts of our white friends whose kindnesses to us th'u the years — in health an' sickness — in happiness an' sorrow — is known to us as bounty in THY SIGHT an' o' THY PROVIDIN' — Amen!"

A rustling of hymnals — a whisper. "Number twenty-fo'!" The Coaster's baton rises, tenses and falls, and an exactly-pitched, mellow harmony swells out in sweetly blended rhythm. "Come 'long t' Glory, on th' far side th' mountains, whar' th' burden o' my sins rolls away, rolls away —" a remarkable tenor, the Coaster's — and Jack's bass, deeper and deeper and truer as the refrain dies away! Spirituals follow, choir and company working itself into the full passion of religious fervor. "An' now, my brethren, sisters, all o' you, lif' up yo' eyes an' hearts t' HIM — t' HIM — a-hangin' up dar on de CROSS. Les' us follow d' Marster, follow him th'u de Ritual o' Jesus at de Well!" The baton is aloft — a volume of "Amens." The Coaster's tenor in solo — he is on his knees now — his perspiring face tense and drawn, his clutching fingers groping into space. "An' dar — HE — hung — an' — uh — HE — uh — looked down — an' says — uh — somebody — please take my po' ol' MOTHER — home." He is on his feet now, darting to right and left, beseeching, exhorting. The gathering swells toward him and the awaited chorus goes throbbing forth. "Yaas — MY LAWD — JESUS gwi' mek up — my

[78]

— dyin' — bed — JESUS gwi' mek up — my dyin' — bed!" Aunt Dora's shrill treble has joined the outpouring. The assemblage is racked with turmoil — on and on — verse after verse of the Coaster's own creation — the Last Supper, the Betrayal, the Bloody Sweat, the Tomb That Opened — the Coaster sinks into an exhausted heap!

Again the yearning to slumber, but somehow the Coaster's ritual comes ringing back, a homely recital that challenges and summons in the very strength of its purity. Jesus will indeed make up many a dying bed in token of such faith. Would that my own —

Jack again with the cedar bucket. Jack with his hot Java. Jack puzzled when the Captain bids him fetch the kodak — the kodak, you know, Jack. The black box in the leather case — Jack's face brightens — picture-making strikes but one sense with Jack — Art. He beams. Identification is complete. "Aw, Cap'n, you means bring you de 'Artry'!" Thus does second nature and native instinct exert a true sixth sense of appropriate designation far beyond expensively coined phrases.

Today we are a cavalcade. Will Joy and his special saddling mule are hard put to it to spy on old Joe. Spruced by his massage and rest, the Old Master cut a dizzy pace. But Nellie slips in with the first find. We miss and locate her behind us in a deep ravine, backbone deep in the wintry sedge, and staunch as the Ark. Hal and Ev descend with satisfactory results when a huge covey roars down the chute and into the dense woods.

Then off on a long and wandering route of Joe's coursing — around hill sides, into remote valleys where another season may pass ere human eyes again peer into such sequestered haunts. Forests, briar-guarded post oak patches, rocky defiles, wafted scents of juniper and sassafras. Open fields, cabin homesteads, the blurr of drifting wood smoke — always the out-rider, Will, searching for the gaunt pointer! The crack of guns spitting through barriers of boughs and grasses — over and over and over again one's poignant gratitude for the given grace of such moments.

But look yonder by the wood's edge. Young puppy Jim, pointing as though his life depends upon it. "Dar he!" yells Will. "I couldn't luv' da' l'il ol' dawg no mo' 'n ef he wuz mah own son. Ef he ain' got birds yu gent'men jes go on an' shoot me down. But ef h'its er rabbit — jes' 'member Jim's youth — an' th' size o' mah fambly!" But Jim comes into his own! "Thirty-two bevies since yesterday morning!" counts Ev, who has done little if any shooting himself. "Twenty-three or four for the old Master — fine work, Old Timer!" And Joe, sensing his work as done, heads over the fields toward Brick House.

Across the windless sheen of approaching noon comes the summons of a bell, from Life Boat Chapel on the hill off yonder, Will tells us. Riders and wagons are heading that way. "De Coaster gwi' preach a sermon dis mawnin' on Gen'ul George Washin'ton, d' Father o' our Country, an' tell all de chilluns dey mus' grow up trufeful." As we swing up through a fence gap and out into a sandy road, a horseman, cantering past, draws rein to bow us a respectful and dignified "Good Mawnin' " — a grave and reverend Coaster, riding into the zenith hour of God's own sunshine, on the mission of Him who makes up *all* our dying beds.

Again Jack and the hay-burners. At the gate of Brick House comes parting of the way for the Colonel and Ev. Blue eyes met grey eyes and two strong hands clasped across the Mason and Dixon line of true sportsmanship in a grip that said as plainly as did words of hearty farewell: "We like you, Yank; you're a good shot and a right man, come back to see us — do!"

"Same to you, Johnny Reb, and more of it. You've treated me white. Long life to you and yours."

"Well," questioned Hal, when our horses' heads were set toward home, "how does the Minute Man from up Boston way like an everyday, Down-in-Dixie bird hunt, with a little Rebel Yell stuff on the side?"

The Gentleman from Vermont sighed a sigh of rich content and stretched wearily in his seat.

[81]

"You are now speaking," said he, with that methodical diction typifying a delineation of accurate verbal juxtaposition characteristic of the ultra-grammatical New Englander, "of the very best thing in the Universe."

"D'm'f 'taint," I echoed softly.

And Hal triple-plated this confirmation in the tongue of our Fatherland.

"Sho' is."

MY DADDY'S GUN

My Daddy's gun! I touch it reverently!
While through a veil that honest tear mist weaves,
Across the years of their brave comradeship,
Drifts comfort in the picture memory leaves.
I see again his stalwart form, and you, old gun,
Both in primal joys of days afield,
When distance dropped uncounted from his manful
    stride,
And all the wealth he sought was Nature's yield.
My Daddy's gun!
Again the glint of golden sedge, an orchard's breath,
And now your voice that echos o'er the hill,
With Bob Whites fled to thicket haven depths,
But left behind — limp, mottled tribute to your skill.
Mirage? No! Sunrise, flooding all the marsh with
    gold!
Cold rain! Swift wildfowl circling to your blind,
Or storm blown snows that beat upon your camp,
"Two souls with but a single thought" — you didn't
    mind.
My Daddy's gun!
Ah! glorious days along a merry, foam-flecked stream,
With all the thrills the Gods o' Luck could send,
To pave a day's path deep in rich content,
Yet dangle greater chances just around each bend.

MY DADDY'S GUN

I feel his arm about me when such days were done,
His 'Little Lad' who trudged along behind,
To share the jest or fun-threat in his level eyes,
And know in them the treasures real Pals find.
No thought of his but leaves your sights held high,
No act of his but leaves you right to pride,
In thirty years of trust and sporting faith fulfilled,
Along the trail to 'Been There', side by side.
My Daddy's gun! I pledge it reverently — again!
That by the living strength and staunchness of
         your due,
Tho' storm blown snows may beat upon our camps,
So will I bear his trust, by you!

ALL OVER GAWD'S HEAVEN

A TREASURED standby of mine is a battered old ledger. Its buckram is threadbare; leather bound corners worn and smelly. Its pages are freckled with brown age-spots and smears from rum and toddy splashings. In my ledger have been set down not cold calculations of profit and loss. No; only crowded jottings from the pleasant yesterdays of some noble sportsmen. Browsing through it of winter nights, I observe dedication as of mid-October, 1882. Notation surmises a railroad's penetrating those regions. Their log cabin will then be replaced by a more modern structure.

Thereabouts, I generally pause, instead of hunting ahead with those jolly "Old Timers." Memories unfold. It comes to me with almost the fragrance of inspiration that during all the years sleeping t'wixt the failing but resolute covers of my ledger, there have been but three secretaries of the Beaver Dam Ducking Club. First, Mister Arthur's sprawling, eccentric fist (he always spelled ducks — dux). Follows the

cramped but precise and neatly shaded penmanship of
the bluff-gruff but lovable "Professor"— the Music
Master. Much page turning and my own boyish hand
takes the club's helm. For the Professor, last of his
group save one, of those grand old men in gray who
drank hearty together and swore no real oath but went
with them to the grave, must needs take up his decoys
at the last sundown, and gently close his locker upon
Life. Hail and farewell to them!

It is reasonable then, for recollections to come first.
Just closing one's eyes and visualizing, for instance,
what that country looked like when access to Beaver
Dam meant a day of Hal's teaming from the upper
Tennessee bluffs, or a night's steamboating down "Ole
Miss" and a stiff mule lug through buckshot and
gumbo jungles. Their "dog-trot" cabin overlooked the
lake's grass-bordered crescent. Even then they deplored
the "inroads of civilization." And they were right.
Alas for whine of saw and thump of pile-driver; clank
and gulp of dredge-boats. Their cabin was turned over
to a Keeper. A rambly, one story, two-room plank clubhouse topped the cane-guarded ridge. And there it
stood, too, until a few seasons ago; sheltering old fashioned double walnut beds, antlers, English sporting
prints, a round-house stove and Hickory-Dickery-
Dock, the big clock. The outfit got a bit shaky on its
cypress pins, and startled looking amid the glare of a

cotton field hiding a former wilderness. The deer and turkeys we hunted close by have been cleaned out from their ravaged habitat. Lakes and swamps sucked dry by logging roads and drainage ditches. A pecan tree, slim sapling in my boyhood days, grew into a huge, shading guardian of Beaver Dam's porch and entry. But in the end it fell victim to a cyclone, and toppling, crushed the club house to smithereens. Nevertheless, to me Beaver Dam endures, just as much mine as since that first stormy night it welcomed us boys (the night a panther screeched and we all three piled into the same bed) and set its stamp on our lives.

I'm telling you this story just as the thing panned out. Again, however, I revert to the ledger; the whole business starts therefrom. Mister Arthur has entered the Minutes of an annual meeting for Beaver Dam. Officers were, of course, renominated and re-elected by acclamation, with reference even to temporary adjournment to "the Frenchman's place." The Professor, Uncle George, Tell, Doctor Robert, Miles, Sam and Bun. The same old bunch! "New business" discloses the necessity for a revised budget. Andrew Jackson Bounds, black club-keeper, begs a salary raise from ten to fifteen dollars the month. Also for permission to charge a dollar for three meals instead of "two-bits" each. Satisfactory adjustment is noted, thereby driving away the wolf apparently at Jackson's door. Then addenda, to wit — "Victoria's annual baby is reported by Jackson last Saturday and promptly christened 'Willie' on Sunday — now and forever more (probably a great many more) — amen!" A bit of a wag and prophet, too, Mister Arthur. So, there's your introduction to Jackson, to Victoria his spouse, and to little "Willie-on-Sunday," as I first saw him about mallard time of 1892, a burr-headed, bowlegged bit of alligator bait of some six chill-infested summers.

There is a pretty little story, or lie, as you choose, in connection with Jackson Bound's coming to the lowlands from the hill country of his birth and upbringing. Rather shrouded in mystery, or rather, one might say, in reluctance of Jackson's confidence as to details. At times, however, the latter was relaxed through assuaging influence of Beaver Dam nutmeg punch, partaken of from many tumbler leavings as the poker game rose, flourished and decayed. Or, once in a great while, alone some winter night and in close commune with the "sperrits" by reason or virtue of having "been borned a twin child," Jackson, from the vantage point of an empty shell case drawn close to Steamboat Bill the Stove, would disclose the impelling secret of his cyclonic migration. At any rate, whatever the truth or merit of the matter, it had made a reasonably devout Christian out of Jackson and his intervaled indulgence in strong waters was accepted as a matter of health

Victoria and a few of her "chilluns"

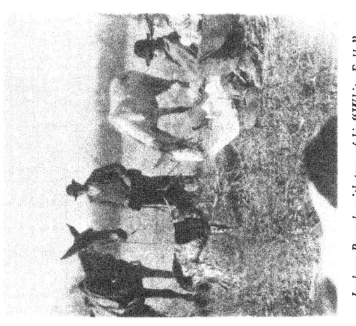

Jackson Bounds with two of his "White Folks"

alone; miasmi in summer, and bitter frosts of winter constituting menaces to be fought off with inward draughts of an outward but spirituous grace. To make a long story shorter, it may be stated here, with due acknowledgement to latter day cults or contentions over ectoplasmic revelations, that Jackson's hasty removal from Hills to Delta was occasioned by a "Hant." It seems that Jackson, following the demise of a carousing comrade, had surreptitiously removed from beneath the latter's dog-trot, several jimmy-johns, used even at that remote period as containers for white mule. Passing along a dusty road in the act of such transport, and accompanied by one Bubbin, a yellow boy, as hireling, they were accosted suddenly at a lonely, moonstruck cross-roads opposite a buryin'-groun', by the deceased, Calvin Brandon by name. Enriched as to bodily outline by a soft glow from the self-same shroud in which a few days previous Jackson had "holp wrop him," Brandon bitterly reproached his friend of former convivial days for bearing off from beneath his house sills, those precious jimmy-johns. And at length the "Thing," having worked itself into foaming fury of gibberish and direful other-world threats, sprang at Jackson and Bubbin. Its bared fangs and talons, according to Jackson, "had growed in the grave." Its tushes, jibing and grating, gave off blue lightning. In revamping this extraordinary experience,

I am fairly accurate in estimating seventy-five miles as separating Jackson's leaving-off point opposite that graveyard and where he pulled up next morning, at Beaver Dam lake. In offering to make affidavit to the above Jackson deposed further to add that the yellow boy, Bubbin, kept pace with him remarkably well for one so young. But canebrakes became moon-high and molasses-thick, and Bubbin once lost to sight, was "nevah heered tell of no mo'!"

Reviewing, therefore, the admitted stimulus involved and allowing consideration for Jackson's recapitulation that "he runned off all but his brogan tops," credulity must needs bow to admiration in his triple Marathonic achievement. So I present Jackson, tall, square shouldered, powerful; a magnificent hunter and tracker; deadly with either Winchester or shotgun. He was quiet, industrious and deeply impregnated with a spirit of loyalty and respect. And what a singer! His basso profundo began in a roar and ended in a rumble, but withal as true and deeply soft as the sea mumblings of a conch shell we children held to our ears for surf memories. Jackson's voice led all others in the little cabin church we club members occasionally attended Sunday nights as specially invited guests to watch the "comin' through" and redemption of some black sheep strayed from the straight and narrow. What a sonorous volume of heartfelt melody swelled through those rude windows. It was "Roll Jordan Roll," "I Gwi' Shout All Over Gawd's Heaven," "Swing Low Sweet Chariot," "Sinner Go Thy Way," and many another such lovely spiritual. Jackson often sang as he poled the bateau homeward evenings, looming heroic against the sunset's red flare paling beyond jagged forest spires. His voice sank then into chanting harmony in perfect accompaniment to swish and lollop of prow water. And as for Victoria, his wife, she might have made sad havoc in a modern kitchen and known little of high-brow culinary art. But with any cook on earth whose offerings extended no further than the fish fry, barbecue, cushion biscuits, and red-peppered, fat-meated dishes grouped under the head of "Potlickers," Victoria held her own and gained the plaudits and affection of all her white folks. How she did fill her kitchen! Her portly "figger" and expanse of roving eye-white bulking against the glowing arc of her fireplace as she ministered alternately to fat-bellied hound puppies and her own "chilluns," with no lack of attention to pots and pans. Another memory is that of three puffed but still ravenous small boys at table with plate after plate of hot brown biscuits going the way of all such amid the wreck of a roast wild turkey and an exhausted molasses jug.

What wood duck shooting we used to have in late summer! Dangerous days, in a way, too. In those times little heed was given window screens, pure water or mosquito bars. A wilderness was being carved — such matters as those could come later — when it was natural to kick out, if death hadn't beaten the carver to it. Our mothers gave us capsules of quinine to take regularly and more often than otherwise we forgot to absorb the medicine. And, promptly on the properly spaced days thereafter, down we'd come with chills and fever. By late August the wood ducks flew strongly. Daybreak on a Delta lake was something exquisite. We took coffee and around three-thirty were hidden in the "yonka pins" or willows before the first faint glimmers of dawn. The whole swamp resounded with a humming tremolo of insect life, racked with the raucous jangle of great blue herons and throaty croaks of myriad shi-pokes. Summer duck shooting, as to results, was largely a matter of proper diagnosis of flight lanes from roost to day grounds and the evening's return flight via another route. Gradually, as half light came, the blue herons were succeeded by swarms of white ones and whirring bands of crimson winged blackbirds, doves and songsters up and away ere the sun. Then came squealing twos, fives, tens or fifties of wood ducks yodelling their day greeting. They decoyed well mornings, if we'd hit the center of their grounds, and we youngsters and our elders popped away merrily. By good sunup it was all over and we spent the hot day fishing for bream, crappie and black bass or napping out under the big pecan trees. Toward sundown, we'd cross Beaver Dam and take stands on the lake bank. The wood ducks, returning to roost, trailed the timber tops, and it was high, snappy shooting. We younglings usually tried some fruitless shots and then stacked arms and went to retrieving before it got too dark. Aye! Those were the days. So, having discovered Jackson and Victoria and little "Willie-on-Sunday," we'll leave them at old Beaver Dam in all their native happiness and content. And now — meet the Judge!

Sometime around the foreshadowing Civil War "sixties," when things began to break rather badly for the Stars and Bars; when there wasn't much of anything left to fight on but parched corn and raw collards once in awhile, and a whole hell's mint of courage that held out gloriously to the bitter end (the better end, after all, bowing to the good Lord's will) — there was a boy's military academy up our southern country somewhere. I've heard the Judge call its name many a time, too. Most all our grown men — and a jag of runaway boys, too — had been fighting for years, and matters had gotten worse off than sure enough desperate, just before that last thrust the Yanks made. Somebody had to try to stop them; to hold up that advance. It's all down in history how those young "wild cats" flew on the job. How school was dismissed

and the cadet drill guns, sure enough capped and slug-
ged, bristled and spat across grim hillsides. The school
cannons grinned and belched a deadly welcome
through red gaps and headlands. And it's just as much
down in history and hearts how many a one of those
half-baked dare-devils died around those same old
pieces but held that precious position until help came
— God bless 'em. And their glory is down in the blood
that came after them and still runs on, quiet and proud-
like and undying and — thank goodness — without
real rancor any more. And some of those lads, after
they'd smelled war powder and looked death squarely
in the muzzle and mocked "eeees" with blundering
minie balls, went on into the melee pell-mell, hurrah
and hell-bent for election. To emerge, at its fag end,
ragged, hungry but rugged "Vets." Oh! they got home
the best ways they could, which meant any old way,
to the folks and fields they loved more than enough to
die for. And how their folks adore them — that is,
what's left of the blood. That's about all there was
left, too, just bare fields, rusted, busted up ploughs,
ragged folks and that same old hell's mint of courage,
faith and love. And there on that stricken and down-
trodden heath of theirs they put up a fight for life and
the ultimate poise of a nation that made Gettysburg
and the Marne look like sham battles. They won, too.
And right in that victory, is where God Almighty

evened up matters on HIS great scales. Set all enemies and their "come-afters" on the right road again with the love of America and the spirit of "one-for-all" in their hearts. Well, that is as good an introduction as I can give you to the Judge. Yes there is, too, one other glimpse I'll let you have of him.

It is May of just a few years back. The "Boys," his boys and many another Daddy's lad and Mother's son, are drifting back to childhood's friendly ways from the maw of the Argonne. From end to end our Main street is a thickset frame of faces. The tears on many of them run the gamut of joy for the living and pity for those whose dear ones are not answering "Fall in," or standing "Retreat" any more in their company streets. Someone shouts "Here they come!" The vast throng stiffens. Standing alongside the Judge and old man Henry Prentiss, looking down from the Judge's office window, I can feel the fine old gentleman tremble and sway. Who knows the drums in his ears from long ago? He swallows hard, catches himself and tries to straighten sagging shoulders. It's there in spirit, that ram-rod down his spine! Away down Main street comes a gust and then — a Roar! Flags and hats and handkerchiefs jumping like bursting grains from a giant cornpopper. They're passing beneath us now! The Mayor, Boy Scouts, and squadrons of police. The regimental band, after a preliminary bugle note and drum tap, turns loose —"Dixie." Of course you couldn't hear your own ears then! Old man Henry Prentiss bleats out a sniggering "Eeee-yawh;" throws an arm about the Judge's neck and yells: "Jim, them boys have sure played Hell now." But the Judge doesn't hear him. He's looking wistfully down at two stalwart figures sitting their prancing horses with an ease that began in boy and pony days. If you could look under those tin hats, and then at the Judge, you'd know his boys mighty quick. And then, after feeling for the tiny shield of Stars and Bars in his coat lapel, to make sure it's there, this moment of moments, the Judge suddenly loses control, clamps a near half-Nelson on old man Henry Prentiss and yelps through the din: "Gawd, Hinry, we may not be wuth a damn as lawyers, but as breeders we have been a monumental success."

But back we go again from there to an afternoon in earlier life to discover the Judge and Jackson shooting wood-ducks in the south end of Beaver Dam lake. He has the "Commander" as guest, and each has a long necked bottle of Catawba cooling in the boat's ice box. I'll let the Judge tell this story, seated, we'll say, in his lean-away-back, creaky desk chair. There are, of course, reflective pauses, loud throat clearings, meditative puffs and wavings of a long ashed cigar. "That particular afternoon, Jackson determined to have me shoot in the Teal Hole. The water was exceptionally low, we — or rather — he had to hunch the boat through the mud and moss. We finally made it, however, and his judgment was as usual upheld by a fine flight. The ducks were crossing heavily and in honor of an impending triumph I took a drink and poured Jackson one, too. He had worked hard. AAAuuummmppphh! Before opening fire, we arranged things comfortably; I am a fiend for luxury as you very well know, suh, doggone you! I then took another sip! I was using that old British gun of mine, but I still attribute my accident to use of that new-fangled powder and possibly a bubble in the weapon's steel. I had knocked down quite a few birds when a fine bunch dropped over the timber. I singled out and fired at a gorgeous drake. The gun seemed to leap from me and my left hand was struck sharply off the fore-grip. For a second or two I neither saw nor felt anything wrong. Then I saw blood spurting from my deadened left hand and numbed arm. Peering closer I perceived blood jets from what remained of my hand, a charred remnant of blackened flesh and protruding, splintered bones. AAAuuummmppphh! Realizing I was seriously wounded, I hastily took a drink! 'Jackson,' I said, 'my hand is shot away — get me to the clubhouse as quickly as you can and call to the Commander as we pass his blind.' Imagine my indignation when Jackson who hadn't as yet seen or realized the situation, replied: 'Yaas, suh, Jedge, I'll pick up de daid ducks an' de m' coys right away!' To which I yelled: 'T' hell with the ducks, nigger, I'm bleeding to death — get me home — you thick head.' Then Jackson saw my hand and the gore. Searching frantically through my shell box for some cord, and not finding it at once, I began to swear, and Jackson to blubber. Tears rolled down his cheeks. When I told him to quit bellowing and find a string, he said: 'Aw, Jedge, how kin' I hep' cryin' wid you fixin' t' die an' cussin' lak dat wid yo' las' bref.' But I found the twine, and, with Jackson's assistance, fashioned a tourniquet. Then began a hard trip. I had waded part of the morass coming in, but I couldn't now. I was getting strangely weak. So I sat down in the boat's bottom and took a drink. Aaauuummpphh! But, Jackson, getting a good grip on the boat's rope, waded ahead, lifting, sweating, plunging and singing. It was a tough business, but he soon had us afloat and paddled desperately. All the while he sang, calling on his Almighty for help. Urged me to 'not cuss no mo'!' He put every ounce of his vast strength into the job and fell back on his religion. When we landed I was what you call 'groggy.' So Jackson simply picked me up in his arms and carried me to a bed in the club room. The Commander came in about that time and rushed his own paddler off for a doctor. He also dispatched a wire for a special train to be rushed down. I had told Jackson before the Commander came to tell him, if I was unconscious, that under no condition was my arm to be amputated until I reached the city, and then only when surgeon consultation said so. I lay in a hazy doze. A country doctor arrived, administered an opiate, ordered boiling water and began to lay out saws and knives. The Commander, alarmed, asked: 'Doctor, what are you preparing to do?' 'To take off his arm, that's all,' retorted the medico. 'But,' remonstrated the Commander, 'the Judge's instructions are to wait until he is home.' 'I'm doing this,' shot back the doctor; 'he'll die otherwise, and I'm going to amputate.' Whereupon, rising to the full austerity of his six feet four and two hundred and thirty pounds, the Commander stated that while he had a great respect for the medical profession, he would be teetotally and eternally damned if there would be anything doing in the amputation line. Fortunately, the special train arrived promptly, and (here the Judge flourishes three remaining fingers of his rawboned left hand) I can still eat, drink, smoke and shoot — in the language of another great American, 'I still live'!"

Years have rolled by since that good day, that is as many as one reasonably minds admitting. Youth, perhaps, gasps at such a spell; but middle age accepts them placidly enough, in fact rather enjoys them if they've been spent trying to do the right thing all along the line. A string of "keepers" have fished and hunted away the interim at Beaver Dam since our generation flew the nest to college and business. Jackson and his brood wandered away when the call got too strong, and Jackson, so the "grapevine" had it, "went to preach-in'." Once in a great while news of him filtered back to his old diggings. Fifteen years or more of silence. Then it was summer duck time again, only the wood ducks of Jackson's day show wide gaps in their ranks. Automobiles, good roads, drainage, autoloaders, pumps and slack consciences and slacker laws have done their deadly work. Only the well meaning and fairly effective arm of Uncle Sam has saved the gorgeous wood duck from extinction.

It has come along to the fag end of a warm afternoon before Confederate Memorial Day. The country doesn't stand still in its honor. To just be walking around town you maybe wouldn't notice much difference. But down in our deep South, banks close and newcomers and irritable new business men may ask "what the trouble is" and go off grumbling about such sentimental hindrances and digging up grievances. But, if you've got the blood in you that clings to the Southern when and why of things, you should know perfectly well what Memorial Day means, Rebel or Yankee stock though you be. We may put on a little more "dog" (as the slang has it) in the cities. But it gets under your skin, city or country. Here and there you'll see an old gentleman toddling along, his shoulder drooped a trifle by the shined up smoothbore musket he's packing, and a worn cartridge box and bayonet belted about an oversize and well spruced uniform of Confederate gray. His little squatty, peaked cap is cocked at identically the same angle he liked to tilt it sixty years ago. They usually fall in around the monument, or their camp's headquarters. Their commanding officer puts them through their manual of arms and then the band strikes up and takes them part of the way afoot, out to the cemetery. They straighten up and get formal and address each other as "sergeant," or "corporal"— bless their dear old hearts! There's always an orator on hand to eulogize the sleeping valiants and those cherished remnants of the grandest race alive today, Blue or Gray! Most of the ladies and girls cry! And on our memorial days years ago Miss Talullah Jenkins nearly always fainted and had to be carried out and be made much over after she'd been revived. Her father, old Colonel Hayward Jenkins, had been the first man over a certain famous breastworks, waving his saber and hollering —"give 'em the cold steel, boys!" Just then a grapeshot took him. And many of us men and boys, looking away through the locusts and magnolias, and the weeping willows and myrtles all

pink against the gravestones, get to thinking about
Gran'pa or Unc' Billy, and remembering what all this
stands for, right or wrong. It isn't a darn thing to be
ashamed of if a film of spider-webby mist creeps t'wixt
your eyes and the sunshine. With maybe a choking
lump holding it there.

Well, anyway, as I was saying, it was the afternoon
before Memorial Day — the Governor of our State
was to be "orator"— when word came to my office that
a colored man wanted to see me. My caller wasn't
shown, he was led in, a tall grizzled old darky. The situation required but a glance. His steering companion,
goggles, cane and that strained, expectant stare of the
blind. The younger colored man, in response to my
look of inquiry, said simply: "Dis is yo' ole club-house
keeper at Beaver Dam — Jackson Bounds." Jackson
Bounds! Faster than radio, memory leaped thirty years
and back again to the patient, wrinkled black face,
wreathing now in a smile whose counterpart he trusted
instinctively must be mantling that of an old white
friend. And he realized, too, that a great, gnarled black
paw thrust timidly forward with that constraint which
embodies the greatest asset the colored race will ever
know, would meet the welcoming grasp of a big little
boy for whom he had toiled in the long ago at Beaver
Dam. And in that fleeting moment, a "cut back"
flashed upon memory's screen. An expanse of broad,

shallow lake, layered with rising frost mist. Blackbirds whirring cloud-like from reed beds. A giant negro smashing hip deep through the cut grass, dragging a duck boat and flinging decoys far across a pond. And then, a lad's first real duck shoot.

It didn't take long for Jackson to explain the "why" of his visit. Three years ago, it seems, Willie, his baby boy (our Willie-on-Sunday) as he called him lovingly, had come to the city from their distant Arkansas acreage, and — alas — fallen foul of "de Law." As Jackson explained it: "He wuz innocent, suh, befo' de good Gawd, but his comp'ny wuz bad, an' de cote jes' up an' fling de limit an' de londy'tude o' de law upon 'im — an' I'se sho' deeply bowed wid de grief o' his 'miliation!" A local family's rare silver plate had been burglarized. I recalled something of the case. Two suspects had been followed so closely that they sought to evade conviction by stopping their car midway of a great bridge spanning the Mississippi and chucking overboard their supposed loot. This the culprits strenuously denied — to be legally specific — they denied it "in toto," stating further, through a colored lawyer wearing horn rimmed glasses and a "ham-knocker" coat, to wit: "That in return for six-bits they had been entrusted with a cargo of 'corn' for delivery to a certain prominent citizen in an adjoining state, whose name, whereabouts, or further connection with the case were, for good of the cause and safety of Willie-on-Sunday's person et al, best left off the docket. That they, the two boys, hearing behind them the siren of a police patrol, and seeing his light so to shine from the bright star cap of a big Police, thereupon did become alarmed, so much so, in a swivet of fear and excitement, they leaped from their carrier and did then and there sling over the bridge's railing said cargo of said 'corn'— that they hadn't stole no silverware — an' didn' know nuthin' 'bout no silver, nohow!"

It was lamentably unfortunate, however, from their point of view and in light of after proof, that the twelve good men and true selected to weigh the evidence, failed to believe this aspect as covered by a denial "in toto." As a result, Willie-on-Sunday and friend had now served their sovereign state for several seasons of an indeterminate sentence. Old Jackson and the other black boy's relatives had followed clues and traced rumors with unflagging zeal, seeking to run to earth the real criminals. Their efforts had at last been rewarded through confession by a shot-down and dying "yegg." He and a pal had turned the trick and the plate was later recovered from a distant "Fence." Thus belated justice stretched out a forgiving hand to Willie-on-Sunday. But even then the path of Justice is mazed with red tape, and with this old Jackson had been unable to cope. He had hunted me out, he said, "becaus' d' ole nigger's white folks is de right folks after all, an' he knowed now he wuz gwi' carry de good word on home t' ole Victoria an' dey wuz both gwi' shout all over Gawd's heaven." Would I help him? Would I? In a jiffy we'd set out for the Judge's office.

Usually, there is little or no formality about getting to see the Judge. His assistants smile and point toward his door, as often as not wide open and the old gentleman reading or arguing with anyone about anything—mostly dogs or ducks or the Civil War. But now there was a formal tone to things. Miss Bessie informed me that "the Judge was entertaining the Governor." But I had ideas about all that myself, and a lurking suspicion that if the Judge knew old Jackson was out there, blind and in trouble about Willie-on-Sunday—why the paramount issues of the campaign or that moth eaten argument about whether Colonel X—— should have brought up his column or not at the battle of the Wilderness — would have to wait. So I asked Miss Bessie to tell the Judge a very old friend wished to speak to him for just a moment, in the private consultation room.

The Judge, responding quickly, looked inquiringly at our odd group. Putting a warning finger to my lips, I crossed and whispered: "He's blind, Judge; give him your left hand to shake — then you'll know each other." Rather dubiously the old gentleman stepped over and extended a three fingered remnant that I steered into Jackson's ham-like palm. "Damn it," exclaimed the somewhat flustered Jurist; "what's all this business about?" The darky's voice was as radiant as his face. Dropping his hickory stick, he clapped his other paw atop his friend's hand, and exclaimed: "Das him — I'se Jackson, Jedge, you don' hav' t' cuss no mo', suh!" About that time I noticed that the Judge had had a snifter or two and it wouldn't take much of this sort of thing to make him choke up, the way he was going on over Jackson. So Miss Bessie and I went in and talked to the Governor. Quite a spell later, the Judge led in Jackson. "Governor," he announced, "this is Jackson Bounds, our old duck club keeper who — who — saved my life years ago when I accidentally shot these fingers off — I'd have bled to death if he — if he hadn't — why — why — this is sure a great all around day isn't it — in two minutes I'll be blubberin' again — he'ah! (to me) get that bottle and those glasses and the sugar out of my cabinet yonder — Miss Bessie you'll excuse or join us — hurry up!"

The Governor listened keenly and more than patiently while the Judge retold this story; argued Willie-on-Sunday's case, charged the jury and put the red tape up to our Chief Executive as stout as it could be put as between "old buddies." "Well, Jim," he replied, and I can see him right this minute, sitting there rinsing his toddy around in his glass and looking meditatively out across the city and our great river, "I'm sorry, Jim, but there's only one thing in the world I can do under the Law and the circumstances."

"Why, hell and damnation, Steve," the Judge began to thunder, "do you mean to tell me"—— but something in the Governor's eye stopped him as the latter continued ——"the only thing I can do is wire in an immediate order for pardon." But I was looking at old, blind Jackson, for his head had drooped and his shoulders that had quivered, straightened with a jerk. "Bless de good Gawd," he quavered, looking up and at us out of eyes that saw a Great Light; "I tol' 'em — I knowed dat all ole Jackson had t' do, wuz fin' his white-folks!"

WHAT RARER DAY?

THE plantation's great bell suddenly crashes the portals of sleep. Protestingly I snuggle deeper into my warm place. On to brazen crescendo clangs reveille to cottonland. From his kennel an old pointer chimes in with dismal howlings.

Lying cozily, I compare my laziness to the alacrity in many a lowly shack and cabin. Lamplight will begin to wink through rag-stuffed window-panes. I catch the ring of axes biting into chop-logs, and sniff smoke from revived ash beds. There will be muffled voices and stable stir; the rattle and clink of agriculture's army going into action. Then it comes to me that for fully forty years I have listened to this same bell "ring out and ring in," as the black folks say. Others, too, from neighboring plantations, have hailed me as I poled an early trail across Big Lake.

Fifteen minutes of stolen doze. Footfalls on veranda steps. A latch turns gently. The guest's presence is respected. I peep as my door opens gently. A huddled

[109]

scuttle-bearer darts to the hearth and applies fire-magic.

"Pomp!"

"Yaas, suh, boss."

"That you?"

"Yaas, suh. Da' me."

"What's it doing out?"

"Kind o' brief lak!"

"How brief?"

"Jes' tol'able."

"Going to rain?"

"Naw, suh, not 'ginst it cloud up."

"It's clear, then?"

"It's clear now, but ———"

"But what?"

Pomp falters. "Ol' Zeb say de moon tips down too far. Say he gwine lay off killin' hawgs till de sign git right."

"Pomp?"

"Yaas, suh, boss."

"Put the coffee pot on the stove and those cold rolls in the oven. Don't monkey with that sausage. Wait till I get there — understand?"

"Yaas, suh."

Another fifteen minutes. I tip-toe, gumbooted, into the warm, spacious kitchen. To Java fragrance I soon add the stimulating reek of frying sausage. Heavy

backstair clumpings announce huge Ab, my negro paddler. After making deep inroads upon the provender, I
abandon rich picking to the onslaught of Pomp and
Ab. Soon I return with shell box and big double gun.
Dousing manor lights, Ab and I strike along an orchard
path leading down the bayou bank to Arthur's duck
boat. Pomp trails, in case of last-moment forgetful-
ness on my part. He hums a love ditty, the refrain of
which is interesting —"Whar' you goin', Adam? I'se
Eve."

"Pomp isn't courting, is he, Ab?"

Ab sniffs. "He call hisse'f."

Ab fills the frail craft aft, and my own bulk forward sags a doubtful freeboard. We nose gingerly
through a strip of open channel in the arrow-grass.

"How much water under us, Ab? About four feet?"

"Better'n dat, boss; mo' lak twenty foot. Don't rock
de boat, please, suh. Dis ain't no mawnin' to dive!"
Then Ab whispers, "Ol' Simmons seed two big al'-
gators down below Life Boat Chapel dis summer. All
dem niggers down dataway scared mos' to death o' de
bayou."

I rearrange even mental ballast. "Run the trails
lately, Ab?"

"Me an' Cap'n done so las' Friday."

"Jump many ducks?"

"Dey was right smart plentiful — yaas, suh."

"What kind mostly?"

"Most gin'ally mallets, suh."

"Can the Cap'n still hit 'em?"

"Well, suh, cose Cap'n he ain't so spry lak; but when dey gives him a fair shot, de ol' gent'man he's jes' as pizenous as ever he was."

The bayou slips its high banks and narrows to an opening in the beetling cypress.

" 'Bout a foot o' watah in de woods," whispers Ab.

We slow down for readjustment before serious business. Eleven years have skimmed by since the last well-remembered day I heaved my own duck boat through this South End muck. Forty years of such swamp scuffling! Ab's paddle jabs us noiselessly up the narrow cut. Speed yields to tense silence. It is legally safe to shoot, but we are jump-shooting. Against the dim background of low visibility, it is futile to grant a leaping mallard overly much leeway. In scant light, once he beats you to the skyline, the chances are in the greenhead's favor.

To our right, from a seldom penetrated morass, rises a mallard chorus. But a sudden, frog-like "me-yamp — me-yamp" to our left makes Ab sink his paddle and hold hard. The call is answered — here, there, beyond! Then I get the talk — of course, gadwalls! Now, I see a black bed of them, crossing the trail twenty yards ahead.

"Gawd A'mighty!" breathes Ab. "Now's de chosen moment. Flat-shoot 'em, boss! Flat-shoot 'em!"

My shoulders heave, but there we crouch, with Ab, I know, bleeding internally. The gadwall raft drifts round a bend. Dawn flicks into day. A startling flight of grisly buzzards skims overhead. Ab gets the pirogue stealthily under way. At the trail's crook, I signal him to stop and rap sharply against the boat rail. A roar from the buck-brush! I have miscalculated and been beaten to the punch — too far over! I glimpse fugitives scattering across timber-tops. But a party of confused stragglers pinches off and lurches too close. The big gun mauls down a pair of drakes! Visions of baconed bosoms, corn-meal dressing and giblet gravy.

Ab chuckles as he hefts the prizes appraisingly. "Dese bullies is fat fo' goodness' sake; but boss, why didn't you slam dem rascals back yondah? Us could've done had de limit wid one bust."

Realizing that an extended discussion of shooting ethics will end at the impasse of Ab's conviction that "a duck in the boat is worth two in the bush," I decline the issue.

"Yaas, suh," agrees Ab solemnly. "Yaas, suh. Da's right; da's right, but mos' o' de gent'mens up at de club dey don't shoot lak you an' Major Ensley does. Dey 'ranges so de ducks lights 'mongst de m'coys, an' when dey do — Great I am! Sometimes dey does say

'Shoo,' but dey says it not very loud, an' it has sho' got to be a swift duck to leave dar twixt de shoo an' de shoot!"

By now the run widens into linked ponds. These open spaces are covered with a scum of seedy duck meat and bordered with button willow. A second smothered roar from around the corner! Ab steadies the boat. I pick them up through interlacing covert, a bunch of suspicious mallards driving for safety. But they must pass our way to clear! I "hunker" down and blaze away. Two birds tumble all awry from among the leaders. My second blast bites off a dismayed climber. Pandemonium! The marsh is in riot! Alarm calls! The surge of zooming pinions! Teal, mallard, widgeon and sprig hover singly and in bunches overhead.

It is, somehow, not easy to avoid shoving shells wrong end first into one's gun. But I manage finally to concentrate, find the combination, and center a pair of easy sprigs. Ab retrieves with mumbles of wonder when the hubbub ceases. "Sho' was some votes in dis district!"

We head up-trail. Tree-tops ahead are mazed with circling birds. I am tempted to stop off a while and call. But the charm of idle jump-shooting is far too potent.

Every shove of Ab's paddle reveals familiar territory. I part the viny overhang of a pond hole hidden amid lofty cypress giants and pause in spellbound reflection. Here, these forty years come November, I saw my first duck brought down. Morning of youth! A shaver, warm beneath the folds of a buffalo robe. Black Jackson is bringing lunch, and me along with it, to a certain gallant gentleman. Jackson thrills me with panther stories, and shows me hawks and eagles as the lazy bateau slips from open water into the brake's somber labyrinth. Closer and closer comes the occasional boom of black powder. We creep to where I now sit wrapped in thought. The screen of life lights in vivid memory. A lone mallard swerves into the picture. The drake's hissed greeting to silent, scattered forms; sunlight glinting from a green velvet head. Faith in nature poised for its rendezvous with fate. A jet of smoke! A crash that sets the crispness dancing! Blue and reddish gray plunging headlong in a crumpled heap.

From a deftly woven hide at the bole of that lightning-struck cypress yonder, a great brown dog challenges watchfully. Out steps a tall, thick-shouldered, dark-haired fellow. Loblolly clings to the calves of his rubber boots. The soft brown of his velveteen shooting coat blends in deadly camouflage with his hiding place.

"Daddy!" I cry, springing crazily to my feet and setting the boat atilt. "Daddy, lemme shoot a duck!"

"I'm as hungry as a wolf!" he shouts. "Bring that rascal here to me, Jackson, an' I'll eat him." Then, as now, I would have died for him.

As we swing about, the picture fades, and in its place I see a youth reading by lamplight in an old log club-house his first treatise on duck shooting. That worn volume, than which he has since read nothing better, is still a priceless possession. How he longed and vowed to follow like trails!

"Watch dat bunch yondah!" warns Ab. "Dey's circlin' disaway!"

Shielded by a fallen pin-oak top, I unlimber my call. Around and around they go. Then, just as conversation peters out from lack of breath, they veer abruptly out of line to investigate my racket. "Now!" I say to myself, pitching up the gun and loosening its starboard charge at that charmed spot out ahead. Rapped head over heels, number one bird hurtles down through splintering branches. Swinging off at a flaring hen, however, I am reminded that pride goeth before a fall. Not a feather!

As we glide through weaving aisles I calculate that I have dropped ducks on well nigh every square yard of this time-worn shooting ground. We have shared — still share — glorious years. The two of us are still hard at it. The reason? Because it has been left just as it was. Because of sporting unselfishness and pride in its maintenance. Because the beauty of nature and wild life meant much to a family of real sportsmen.

Thinking all this, I tell myself that any proper visualization of duck shooting must include a background of reminiscense, a foreground of its modern administration, and an estimate thereby of its future, as affecing recreation, industry and national character.

Morale in shooting has become superficial. The flavor and romance which graced old-time shooting standards and companionships among gentlefolk are being forced to wave the white flag to protuberant boorishness. Natural resources in both birds and habitats are being wasted through the rape of ill-devised drainage and delay by haggled interests of research and appropriations. We vaporize amid unsolved weather cycles; we temporize with raw political expediency. Hunters increase. Dizzy transportation facilities give access to remote sectors.

We are drifting faster than we even dream toward a sterility in wild life of the marsh and upland, from which there will be no returning. The pace must slacken! How truly has it been said that "as a nation allows itself to lapse into a condition of sophistication, irresponsibility, materialism and other resultants of luxury and wealth, it loses its place in the sun. Slowly it is supplanted by other nations, hardier, more vigorous and more moral."

But by now our prow strakes are asplash. Big Lake, stretching away northward into the fog, gives off only the wrangle of distant, rafting coots. My eyes travel the winter-stricken circle of forest. Recollection grips again. Yonder, a husky of twenty, home for Christmas holidays, I had a narrow squeak.

One bitter dawn I managed, by some lucky maneuvering through the ice, to outstalk a gang of roosting geese. Glowing with the excitement of a successful right and left, I jammed my boat in the stumps and waded off across an open pocket. Retrieving the first honker, I flung it behind me and made for my second victim. The water, first calf and then knee-deep, began sloshing my thighs. It was no morning for wet feet, but youth rarely kens restraint. With stunning abruptness, I stepped off into space. The water, so cold it actually burned, closed over my head.

Emerging in a paroxysm of anger and fear, with shell-laden coat dragging me down, I grabbed at some drooping willow strands. The slender withes tore through my fingers — broke! I saw them whip upward as I sank! Coming up, I seemed to time their lashback. My lunge caught firmer strands and held. There I clung until a careful knee-hold eventually enabled a crafty wiggle from the death trap. Then I stood up and, with clothes stiffening, loudly reviled such luck. On a platform stand near by I built a rousing blaze, stripped, and dried out as best I could. Then I resumed, without ill effect, the serious business of the day.

But scarcely have Ab and I re-entered the trail when

two dainty duck shapes whir into the air! In the ensuing millionth of a second's trigger pause, it flashes over me how many times hereabout I have had this same opportunity to score double on teal. The straight, thick gun comb shoves both eyes beyond a tilting guide-sight, wilts the escaping right-hand bundle of green and brown, and levels off in search of number two. It is a patchy scratch, but we find him, stone-dead.

On the home stretch we take our time, "turning" a squirrel or two while accumulating an easy limit. And so we come, about mid-morning, to the end of a perfect jump-shoot. Carefully, with decks awash, we negotiate the alligator water.

Ab cocks an eye at the sun. "Whut you say us rides ovah to de rivah, boss, an' try dem geeses? Mister Arthur says he seed a whole passel o' dem over dar las' week."

A second attack upon hot coffee and country sausage. Some pony-express mule saddling by Pomp. High noon finds us breasting the great levee's ramp and dropping down again into the black gold of riparian wilds.

Landmarks crowd up for greeting. The old commissary is a flood-swept, jack-strawed ruin. Even the road has changed. We are forced to circle a quarter-section of sloughed woodland — mighty trees gone the way of all grandeur. But a tottery log cabin still clings to the bank. What a change in the sand-bar itself! In earlier days its white expanse cut sharply from the caving escarpment of Harbert's Bend. Thence it bellied north a full three miles toward the Harding light. Across, behind the bar's loftiest plateau, lay a cut-off section of the old river bed. What black mallard shooting we used to have in there on windy days with a rising river! . . . . .

Westward hissed the furious main channel, the rise and fall of its insatiable gnaw spitting spume and drift over gravel and reefs. Bar change is an old story to the veteran goose hunter. Old Man River has a way of not letting his right bank know what his left doeth — that is, until he gets good and ready. First he coats a lower bar tip with silt, gradually building fields of soft, treacherous mud blocks sprouting grand goose feed in the form of tender young switch willows. Then, all at once, some flood scours out a whole bar, tumbling it down river, to be reorganized miles below. Thus, a plantation owner gains or loses hundreds or even thousands of acres of fast-growing cottonwoods, revetting willows and crop lands, to say nothing, incidentally, of goose bars and duck sloughs.

Ab shoulders decoy pack and shovel. We thread Arthur's path, slashed through half a mile of slender willow stalks. "A school marster sho' would be in de Promised Land wid all dese switches to grab from," ruminates my companion. There is something reminiscently callous in Ab's simile.

We emerge upon a wide bar. The distant river, lower than I have ever seen it, is a mere gash. Barely audible from far below, lilts a high goose note. Ab grins as he lowers the profiles and begins spading. "Dey done give deyselves away, an'," shading his hands to peer across the river, "yonner's some mo' struttin' roun' on dat long p'int."

I am soon correctly dug in and stooled. We confer on the stalk.

"I'll ease into de willers, boss," plots Ab, "an' sneak to de low end o' de bar. Den I'll slip out an' git below de geeses an' try to start 'em disaway. You know, boss sorter rounst aroun' wid 'em."

If agreeable to the "geeses," the plan is quite clear and has my hearty endorsement.

Shouldering his one-hammered double-barrel, in case, as he puts it, "sumpin' mout rise up outa de bushes an' flounce onto him," Ab soon disappears beyond the dunes. Mid-afternoon sunshine hangs in surrender to the chill of expectant waiting.

My eyes travel a panorama of dun shore-line. Where I now stand was mid-current of the Mississippi five years ago. Those tree-tops away off there mark the Indian mound's magnificent oaks. The chances are they saw empires change hands. Beneath them, year after

year and with Horace to help, my wife and I pitched
the goose camp. In memory, the gleam of our fire
beckons. We slog toward it, heavily laden and in biting
darkness. I strain to lift the heavy yawl up-current. I
feel the rip of whirlpools, the smother of heavy chop
with its sickening sense of disaster left just behind. I
hear the patter of rain on our canvas; the frantic
bluster of night winds; the clanging din of voyaging
goose music trailing into the maw of starlight. I live
again the days around our stew kettle with its savors
of duck, goose, quail, fish and what-not. Jimmy and
Don find bevy after bevy amid the corn and wild peas.
The jungles yield tribute of muscadine and persimmon.
Whimpering hound pups catch primer scent from
"varmint" spoor in the night tangles. . . . . .

Back talk from the goose precinct arouses me from
reverie. Excited gabbling joins the watchman's higher
flutings. Suddenly I fancy I catch the thump of lifting
pinions. Righto! A black mass winks over the bar para-
pet. By George, Ab's stalk may bear fruit! They'll
hardly take to the river this late. The dark spot writhes
into a dotted line against the sky. By the tin ear of the
great jinx, they're fixing to cross out my way! Something inside me as old as life and younger than youth
zig-zags from spine to hair-roots.

On they work! A slit twixt pit rim and a decoy belly
shows that our set is spotted. With my back to the

breeze, I am concerned only with the big moment. Is it a straight decoy or just a veer? To do business, or a hasty look-over and fare-thee-well? My eyes read sign through the peep-hole. Excited chatter is suddenly hushed. That has a meaning all its own. No decoy! Their flight is too strong and steady for a slide-in, but they're not disturbed and will cross over me not twenty yards high.

A great black and white shape fills my upturning eyes. The masked muzzle slips evenly past it and erupts. *Wha—am!* The victim blurs as I leap to my feet and swing on to a frantic climber. Reeling under the heavy impact, he slants out of control and crashes in a flurry of sand. It is fast coming sundown. From a distant speck Ab materializes, waves congratulations and retires knowingly beneath a snag root. Flocks of ducks, lazily spending the day on the river, strike courses to roosting lakes inland. I decide to gamble fifteen minutes against picking-up time.

Ab whistles shrilly. Good Ab! My eyes devour the Bend, high — low. Ah-ha! Five geese from off the cross-river point! I shiver, wet my lips and stare in almost unbelieving gratitude. They are over our bar now — rising, sinking. Yes, they've seen our profiles! Guttural "alunks" break out! I understand that kind of talk, too!

"Lay off them guys!" the squad sergeant is saying.

"I don't like their looks. Step on it, File Closer, an' no back talk! We've five miles to do to Kirby's cornfield."

"Give us a break!" grunts File Closer. "I think I know a gal in that outfit. Gee, but you're tough! Have a heart, Sarge!"

"Oh, all right, buddy, but not too close," growls Sarge, winging a slight left oblique that is really very much against his seasoned judgment.

I hurl both tubes of fours out across space. Good-natured, gruff old Sarge, his canny neck gone suddenly limp, has led his last detail across the cleanest highway.

Ab comes running. We sack the shadows. I am thinking, while we backtrack and board our patient mules, that another rarer day has been vouchsafed me. Such, I reflect, is divided into anticipation, participation and, best of all, memories. Fire-log and impending grub call are vanguard to dreams. To rig decoys, tune one's call or stow plunder against the clock's urge is wine to the blood. To mush fair going or foul, to gauge wind or lead, is to reach as fine a skirmish line as God's outdoors affords.

We top the levee. Wrapping my weather-beaten old mackinaw more closely, I settle deeper into the saddle and turn in fervent blessing and *au revoir*. The west is a mêlée of brilliance. Far-flung ensembles of pink and purple expire against an ice-blue east. And as it all sinks gradually from view, some unseen hand repaints life's dearest picture. Fire-glow and student lamplight tussle the shadows of a book-lined chamber. A sweet-faced lady reads *Oliver Twist* to a sleepy lad at her knee. Beside the boy, dreaming his own dreams, is stretched a great brown dog. And close by, busily engaged in polishing the chaste side locks of a beautiful gun, sits Brown Velveteens!

Aye, what rarer day?

MY DOG—JIM

One of five from his royal line; one of four — then
three,
One with strength to carry on; and Jim was spared
to me.
Puppy days! Oh! puppy days! Potlicker, rabbits and
fun,
From dewey dawn to locust's song, nothing to do but
run!
'Member your first school days, Jim? Your first keen,
birdscent thrill?
When you spotted the Colonel's pet bevy, over the
cedar hill?
And how you chased that "cotton tail" that led you
through the ditch,
And how you took your medicine, when I came, with
the switch?
Didn't the years pass happily, while we hunted on
together,
Across the hills and dales of Life, in any old kind of
weather?
I can see you sprawling in the hall, of our old plantation
home,
With its vista of golden acres, that were kingly yours
to roam.

MY DOG JIM

*Sure no monarch ever flagged his plumes with prouder
caste or grace,*
*Nor champion's heart bore cleaner crest, upon a real
friend's face.*
*Ah! how you leaped at sight of gun, and my tattered
shooting coat,*
*Then flashed far out beyond my horse, with dog's joy
note, in your throat!*
*No day too long, no way too hard, nor toil, nor ice too
thin,*
*For you to work your heart out, and always work, to
win!*
*Sundown days! sundown days! Brave hunting thews
grown old,*
*But your champion's blood still urging; your noble
heart still bold.*
*When I've found my life's last covey, and my horse
turns back, to where*
*They count life's bag and pay off, in specie of your
share,*
*If they hunt through fields out yonder, or on through
regions dim,*
*When he hears our old time whistle, why then, I'll see
"Ole Jim."*

PLAY HOUSE

"Oh! happy Boy; you have not lost your years,
You lived them through and through in those brief
days
When you stood facing Death! They are not lost!
They rushed together as the waters rush
From many sources! You had All in One!
Why should we mourn
Your happiness? You burned clear flame, while he
Who treads the endless march of dusty years
Grows blind and choked with dust before he dies.
And dying, goes back to the primal dust
And has not lived so 'long' in those long years
As you in your few, vibrant, golden months,
When, like a spendthrift, you gave all you were."
(Anonymous).

COUSIN CHARLEY and I had figured to turn the hunt
homeward. Quite a piece it was, too, across those hard-
wood ridges, pine domes and sedge hollows that made a
skyline for Big Hatchie basin. Leo and Tom Cotton

were off on cast. We trudged across the furrowed aisles of a rustling corn patch, and found them both staunchly on birds, just where a curlycue broom's end of weeds plaited in among thinning stalks.

Leo was strictly in character, head and plume aloft, dog aristocracy posed and poised. Brawny, lumbering pointer Tom, having evidently swung offhill a trifle late, was bowed into an upstanding study in rigid, pop-eyed liver and white. Since that good day, almost a quarter of a century ago, the memories of those two valiant comrades and that particular happening, have never left me. Their like comes about once in a life time, and perhaps rightly so.

Leo belonged to Billy Joyner, and Tom Cotton to me. But in those brave days shooting interests were so unselfishly interlocked that dog sharing was an indissolubly companionate affair. Leo had handled chickens from the Texas Panhandle to the wild-rose hedges of Saskatchewan. Many a time he had stopped to stare at the dust trails of antelope. And fight? He and Tom met in many a sanguinary set-to at catch-weights. But their issue, whatever it was, was never definitely settled. Sometimes Tom took the count and limped pitifully for days. Again, it was Leo who licked gaping gashes in his burr-curdled hide. From kennel to bird field in baggage car or buckboard, the air was electric with intoned mutters and snarled dares. Once thrown down on the job, however, and stretched out for a day's business, no more friendly or loyal brace of comradely cooperators ever spoored an upland or fought tooth and toe nail in common cause.

Many a mob of snipe-snouted, shaggy mongrels have I seen surge forth and wolf down upon Leo and Tom. And just as often their frenzied yowls of impending mutilation would suddenly crescendo into notes of dismay as "our boys" met them more than half way and filled the impromptu arena with whirling casualties. They had a way, too, of travelling meekly past some rural danger zone, one in front as a skirmishing decoy, the other lagging warily in support behind our horses. Out would bluster some chunky, coarsepelted bully, fat, meaty tail awhirl and ruff abristle, cocked and primed to swarm all over the apparently shrinking and submissive stranger. Camouflage and ambush! Apparently from thin air, a very devil incarnate in dog hair would suddenly fasten upon Shep's unprotected flanks, nosing for a rib-smashing roll-over and the deadly paw hold. And sometimes it required apologies and peace offerings of cash after such flurries. But, their day's hunting done, Leo and Tom immediately resumed their private feud.

Well, that's how we came on them that particular afternoon. I was on the left, with left-handed Cousin Charley beside me. A segment of tumble-down rail fence 'twixt us and the birds. And a sign "NO HUNT-ING" tacked to a near-by persimmon tree. Funny how one remembers such things, but that was the setting. It had been an altogether gorgeous day. Lunch time almost before we realized it. We found a sunny spot just off Fish Trap dam and lazied on the pine needles, while we munched well-browned soda biscuits and lardy spare-ribs. The Big Hatchie is a rare sight from the eminence of Fish Trap. It comes curving and slush-ing past an arrow-headed island, above where the dark-some Sally Hole Swamp juts its fist of cypress into the river bottoms among the hardwoods. Then it fans into a sheet of greenish black enamel with a habit of switch-ing to lumpy amber when heavy thunderstorms scour the seamed faces of the basin's red headlands.

But up and on our way again! It was ideal bird find-ing time when we broke out atop that hogback and slanted down in search of our dogs. Our shooting coats were bulging toward completed quotas—larger then. Another find or two meant finis. We paused in dis-turbed contemplation of the "NO HUNTING" sign.

Cousin Charley grunted. "Got 'em sure as shootin', but that's jus' exactly what we kain't do—shoot."

"Why," I questioned, balancing gingerly on a rot-ting rail and peering past him at Tom and Leo, sculp-tured against the dun swale, "how come we can't shoot?"

"Ol' man Pomp Eddins' place—tha's 'how come'—see that sign, don't you—well, he means it."

"Who th'—who is Pomp Eddins—mus' be hard boiled." Cousin Charley clucked tongue and cheek mournfully. The situation was ruinous. "Ol' man Pomp Eddins," he explained gravely, "is one o' them kind o' ol' gent'mans h'it don' do no good t' fool with —tha's all."

"Bad actor?"

"Well, naw, not 'zact'ly a bad actor, but if he gits in behin' you f' good cause, he'll jes' natcherly run you right on 't degredation — an' we're a long ways from home t' start runnin'—too."

"Can't we ease around an' drive those birds off his land?"

"Might, but I guess we better not—ou'h folks an' Mister Pomp has always bin ve'y fren'ly—but I ain' presumin' nuthin'—they tell me folks that does don' have no luck."

To the infinite consternation of Leo and Tom, Cousin Charley quietly flushed a bevy that scattered enticingly on a hillside not far away. Cousin Charley, as shooter and host, was using his wits. "Now then," he grinned, "le's go to th' house an' as't his permission to shoot a few birds on his place—I know him well enough t' do that—an' we ought to, anyhow."

We struck off up a winding road. "I know right

where them birds lit," remarked Charley. I said I did, too. "I ain' seen Mister Pomp in quite a spell," he went on; "him an' papa wuz in th' Confed'rate army t'gether—but th' ol' gent'man is mighty queer." Leo and Tom, sensing as dogs have a way of doing, that the hunt had taken an odd turn, were in at heel. Charley told me more of Mister Eddins. Retired now, he used to keep store in town—president of the bank once upon a time. Knew some of Billy's and my kin-folks in the city. "If he lets us shoot we can git cleaned up all-fired quick," concluded Charley.

The twists and turns of our way mounted higher among coniferous knobs. "Great folks, them Eddinses," puffed Charley; "th' Civil War 'bout cleaned them up —clan seeded down t' ol' man Pomp; but he kep' things t'gether—don't owe no man—an' had a sight o' cash money an' sev'ul hundred acres—yep—daughter-in-law an' grandson—always been 'folks' an' still are, them Eddinses." We walked out into a clearing. Deeply set amid holly and cedars squatted an antebellum, white brick cottage, its wide chimneys giving off squills of wood smoke into the keen sunshine.

It was young Mrs. Eddins who ushered us cordially into the cozy vastness of a low ceilinged chamber, filled with crowded book shelves, hair sofas, arm chairs and a grandfather clock that would have made a collector's acquisitive hair stand on end. She spoke gently to a tall, gray haired, angular old gentleman who unwound from a deep rocker. "Daddy, here's some company come t' see you." Cousin Charley stepped forward: "Mister Eddins, this is Charley Johnson; good afternoon, suh!"

"Yes," he acknowledged gravely, his eyes meanwhile measuring us both in rapid appraisal, "I know you well, Charley; h'its bin som' time sence we met howsomever. Yo' folks all comin' 'long all right I hope?"

"Yes, suh, Mister Pomp — uh — Mister Pomp — this is — uh — Mister Buck'inham — from down in th' city — comes out bird shootin' onc't in awhile. Ou'h dawgs got into a covey down yonder on th' brushy side o' yo' place, but we seen yo' posted sign an' come on up t' ast if you'd mind us a shootin' a little if we run into another bunch on ou'h way home — we're meanin' t' head thataway."

Mister Pomp's keen eyes, deeply recessed 'neath shaggy brows, swept me from head to foot. He slowly extended a leathery, man's-sized hand. "Buckingham — is it?"

"Yes, suh."

"Gran' son o' ol' man Henry?"

I nodded.

"He wuz frum th' Nawth — an' sided that way."

"Yes, suh."

[135]

"But his brother — yo' great Uncle Fred — he went out fu'st with Walker an' got set with th' Federals — crossed under a flag o' truce at midnight when his term expired second day o' th' battle o' Fredricksburg, an' re-enlisted under Lee — transferr'd later to th' Louisiana Wildcats — they blowed him up on th' Queen o' th' West." I listened in amazement. We had quickly gotten down to rock bottom on party platforms.

A moment of hesitant recapitulation by Mister Pomp.

"Which one o' ol' man Henry's boys is yo' Daddy?"

"Miles."

"Ummm — in th' bank?"

"Yes, suh."

"Th' two younger boys — Gunn an' Hugh — in th' dry goods business — they yo' uncles o' cose?"

"Yes, suh."

"Well, I didn't hav' no better fren's than them boys — all o' them — back in th' hard times panic o' '93 — they carried me — took care o' me an' mine." His brilliant eyes turned from piercing scrutiny of me off through the window toward the Basin's distant rim. A resurgent sun poured over it. He quidded rapidly. Another line of evidence must be established. He said:

"Yo' wife's folks wuz th' ol' Cap'n Joneses, warn't they?"

"Yes, suh."

"Ummnn — tho't I heard tell — Jones wuz my Cap'n — fought all over his own lan', too — Yankees, rich 'uns f'um up Nawth own it now an' fine folks they are, too, I'm told." He spat explosively into the fireplace.

"If I rec'llect rightly, yo' wife's a gran' niece o' ol' man John Jarratt's ain't she?"

"Yes, suh." No use to elaborate; best to stand hitched and come clean.

"John an' me done som' tall ridin' an' shootin' t'gether — we wuz' with Forrest. On'ct in awhile we had t' do som' all-fired runnin', too." An aquiline nose twisted into a grim snicker at the recollection. Half reverie apparently swept us from his thoughts. Then, "You boys take chairs, git warm — you're welcome t' shoot on my lan' whenever you choose — I'll jes' go 'long with you a piece t'day — I ain't shot at a bird in fifteen yea'hs — John — John Yancey — aw — John Yancey!"

A rough and tumble specimen of shaver hardihood, with clear gray eyes and mop of tousled red hair, darted in from the hallway. The grandfather's eyes blazed with pride. "Say 'howdy' to th' gent'men — say 'howdy,' John Yancey — then run an' fetch Grandpa's gun."

With a whoop of joy the little fellow sprang away and soon returned lugging an old but beautiful muzzle loading shotgun. It was in superb condition — muzzles paper thin, locks that sang like harpstrings; stock fit and balance that made shoulder spot and eye all one. With it was handed up belt, powder horn and shot pouch. A genuine Manton!

"Git yo' hat, John Yancey,— you an' Grandpa's goin' bird huntin'— I want you t' watch these good shots an' learn how t' hit 'em, boy — you'll be needin' some such knowledge one o' these days." There was a method in Charley's madness as we retraced that quarter of a mile to the vicinity of our scattered birds. They had moved around an orchard's rim just outside some splash pine. Tom nailed them tightly. I believe to this good day both he and Leo had an idea what was up.

How I wish more of today's "sports" with magazine guns could have watched that old gentleman hustle his percussion Manton into action. In my own boyhood I had, of necessity, performed a like manual, but with nothing remotely comparable to his exhibition of rapid and orderly precision. Nipples capped, he stepped forward and to the left. Charley spun one victim from the rise. But old man Pomp Eddins laid down a bang-up right and left that served notice how he played the game. Congratulations over, we followed the singles across a gully and into a patch of low broom hedge, where we found both Tom and Leo on point.

"Do you boys mind," queried our host, "if I let this

little chap try t' see kin' he hit a quail on th' wing —
he's shot a few rabbits an' some squirrels, settin'—but
this'll be his firs' chance flyin' — an' over a dawg?"
He turned and smiled at the grandson —"come on —
boy." The Manton, recapped and hammers drawn,
was thrust into the lad's eager hands. All must go well
with Grandpa there to see it done. Gun below the
elbow, keen for contact with a long awaited moment,
he braced for the rise. In every gunner's life, in every
father's heart, there should be, at least, one such undying memory.

"Walk on in — walk right on pas' th' dawg — when
th' bird gits up — take yo' time." Step by step the child
obeyed leadership. "Both eyes open, John Yancey, pick
yo' bird an' keep both eyes jes' on him."

Singles took leave on every hand. I can still see that
broth of a boy, stockinged calves and butternut knee
breeches spraddled into a resolute stance among the
sedge stems. Determined arms slamming the burled
stock — a long pause as the child levelled and swung.
B-o-o-m — b-o-o-m. A boy on his knees peering beneath a smoke screen, an old man's shrill cry, "you got
him, son, you got him!" A race through the grass as
youth and old age broke shot for the retrieve! Oh! the
radiance on their faces! Pomp's aglow with pride; the
boy's alight with the greatest thrill any possessor of
game heritage treasures as no other in life.

[139]

For the next half hour neither Charley nor I fired a shot. Then, borrowing the Manton, we took turns at finishing our limits with the tool of a vanished field gentility.

Gulch bottoms were beginning to darken. Shadows thrust claws across the Basin. The crest of a steep ridge split away cleanly, dropping almost a hundred sheer feet to the railway gash. Behind Mister Pomp, we followed a well defined trail across the hump. It ended in a spacious alcove, swung like a dirt dauber's nest above the brink. I looked about me in wonder! Some grim business hereabouts! Pomp Eddins slackened pace and motioned about him. "I tho't mebbe you'd like t' see h'it." He placed the Manton carefully aside and seated himself on a lichened boulder. "There wuz big doin's went on he'ah — big doin's back in Shiloh times." Mister Pomp smiled reflectively. "I'll bet Charley ain't ever bin in this spot befo' in his life — y'see — from he'ah this height commands th' railroad plum across't th' Basin — from whur' th' ol' M. & C. comes outa th' far gap." Somehow he seemed to kindle, take fresh grip on himself. He lapsed into the speech of ancient action; words of almost broad patois leaped from him —"this he'ah wuz an ol' fo'te — I hepp'd build h'it — look yonder at them timbered bastions stickin' outa th' groun'."

He glanced ruminatively at worn, angled earth-

[140]

works and crumbling casemate. Lethargic burrows in their aged blanket of peaceful silt and grasses. "We wuz dismounted an' order'd on detail t' mount two pieces — told t' hold this position at any an' all cost. H'it warn't no easy job, young men, gittin' them guns so high — but h'it wuz wuth th' labor."

His eyes snapped fire; he was at work again. "We come in from behin'— aroun' yonderways — lak we come while ago — with an infantry company in suppote fuh ambush."

I visualized that scene. Gaunt, dog tired gunners in ragged gray. Slobbery, lathered horses, sputtery whip lashes, straining traces, laborious heaving through steamy morass and unaxed swamp. What a beehive of slap-dash, slaughterous activity and toxic hate. A steady voice continued: "I 'member how we stopped 'em th' fust time — a supply train with guard — we wuz hid out an' ready when their locomotive come th'u th' gap and pulled jus' onta that trussle y' see down yonder. We had it blocked with logs; they seen 'em jus' in time as they run outa th' curve. We let 'em git out an' start unloadin'— then we cut that injin' t' ribbons — blowed h'it t' Hell-an'-Gone." He leaped to his feet and almost swarmed to a counter-attack — "Ou'h boys swung ovah th' hill an' flanked 'em — some tried t' make h'it away th'u yon' valley," he chuckled, "but h'it warn't no use — we — we —

had 'em — them hillsides yonder wuz strew'd with dead." He was telling it to High Heaven! "We sho' raised Cain in these parts fo' mo'n two months — but fin'lly th' Yanks come in fo'ce with heavy guns an' shell'd th' livin' hide offn us — we — we — had t' abandon th' position and fall back — damn it."

I looked about me more carefully. Through worn embrasures grinned two dummy cannon, fashioned from pine logs painted black and mounted upon hewn wooden gun carriages. About them, in orderly stacks, were piles of round shot — mud balls! As I half grasped all their significance, the flaming realism of this old man's passion and adoration gripped me. I saw sweating, unshaven half-madmen lashing back on lanyards; blistering hands fumbling at red hot gun muzzles; hell-and-damnation curses turning peaceful quail country into a sudden shambles of thudding smooth bores. Mister Pomp caught my look and smiled grimly. "This he'ah," he injected half fancifully, "is whut me an' John Yancey calls ou'h 'Play House'." He dropped a comradely arm about his grandchild's shoulder. The child cuddled lovingly against him.

"Y'see," he went on, a proud sort of wistfullness creeping into his tone, "y'see, I had t' raise this chile — me an' his Ma — that is — we come t' this ol' fo'te when he wuz jes' a babe — in m' arms — h'it come t' me one day t' fix things up lak' you see 'em — I jus' built it all in mem'ry o' them times — an'— an' as John Yancey growed up, we jus' kep' comin' an' addin' t' things." His jaw suddenly tightened — he spoke proudly: "Anyhow, this he'ah ain't no bad Play House t' bring a boy up in." John Yancey spoke up, softly: "Gran'pa, we hav' a lot o' fun he'ah, don't we?" The old man turned to me. "I fought — we all o' us fought," he cried passionately," f' ou'h conception o' home an' rights jus' as t' other side seen their'n — my father fought in Mexico, I fought with Forrest — an' — an'—this chile's Daddy — th' only son God HIM-SELF could ever give me — wuz killed at San Juan Hill — he couldn't no mo' astayed at home when th' call come, than John Jarratt coulda' hep'ped ridin' off with us boys."

We shook hands and exchanged "good-byes" and "come agains." He said simply: "Tell all yo' folks y' met ol' man Pomp Eddins — yo' Daddy'll 'member me — sen' me a bird dawg puppy some time — I'll train him an' John Yancey t'gether — John's gittin' too big f' th' Play House anyhow." So, leaving them to turn back across their darkening trail through the hills, Charley and I slid down a precipitous path to the railroad ties and a starlit trek to home.

Fifteen or twenty years is a long, long time! Again, however, Cousin Charley and I munched soda biscuits and hog meat at Fish Trap Dam. The bottomlands

still challenged change, but it was there, however furtive. The drone of an aeroplane might impeach the
years, or some raucous motor change the face of things.

"Charley," I asked, "whatever became of the old
gentleman way back over yonder across the Tubba —
Mister Eddins, who knew my folks an' let us hunt on
his land an' showed us his old Rebel's 'Play House'?"

"Daid," responded Charley, laconically; "he lived
t' be pas' eighty — but he passed away aroun' Christmas time — didn' las' long after th' Worl' War."

"And the boy," I went on; "I suppose he turned out
to be a bum bird hunter, like we are, and runs the old
home place now?"

"Yep," replied Charley, and something in the way
he spoke it made me look up. "There was sho' one
mighty fine, honest-t'-Gawd boy, too."

"He's——?"

"Yep!" Cousin Charley was a direct narrator.
"They hadn' no sooner started talkin' war with Mexico, back in '16, but what John Yancey an' his Gran'pa
showed up in town with John's gripsack all packed.
That kid signed up an' went on out with th' National
Guard — an' I mean he lef' out right now." I might
have guessed as much. Cousin Charley loosened a rib's
end and kept on with his story. "Then, y' know, come
sho' nuff war — with Germany. By that time John
Yancey had turned out t' be a natcherl born soldier —

his Grandad darn near passed out, he was so proud when th' boy went to an officer's training school an' come out with a commission. I never seen no one quite as happy. Why — why — there wuz times he'd talk about h'it an' tears'd come to his eyes. John Yancey's wuz a first unit overseas, too."

Charley paused. Tossed a welcome shred of fat meat to a dog. "Ol' man Pomp Eddins come t' town a lot in them days — wanted news 'bout th' war, an' that boy, mebbe. He'd sit aroun' in a big swivet 'till he got his mawnin' paper off th' 'Cannonball'— talked about how he wish'd he could'a bin along with John Yancey. That ol' man meant ev'y word he said, whut's mo'. He'd say: 'this he'ah makes fo' wars f' us Eddins — fo' wars an' th' Lawd only knows how many mo'. John Yancey — he'll be comin' home befo' long — an' — an' — marryin' off'."

A flock of ducks suddenly dipped through the chute and whizzed across the spillway. Cousin Charley grabbed his gun and sorrowfully watched them dwindle into specks. He loved to sneak mallards and jump them around bends. He went back to his story.

"I happn'd t' be at th' sto' th' night th' tel'graf operator brought up th' message 'bout John Yancey. Somebody jus' had t' ride out an' git th' news to his folks. So I run out in m' car — they'd done gone t' bed long ago. But ol' man Pomp he come to th' do'h with a lamp in one han' an' that ol' muzzle loader o' hisn' in t' other. He seen h'it wuz me an' says, 'why — com' in, Charles,' says, 'glad t' see you — my daughter'll be right he'ah. Whut you got — a message fo' us 'bout John Yancey winnin' another medal o' honor,' says, 'how many Germans is that boy done kilt this time?'

" 'Bout that time, his Ma, Mrs. Eddins come into th' room — I guess I musta looked kinda' funny — maybe h'it wuz whut they call 'mother's intuition'— I don' know — guess she jus' sorter suspicioned — you know? All I could do wuz jus' han' her th' War Department's telegram — you 'member how they wuz worded?" Charley looked at me, and remembering, turned quickly away. He hadn't meant to put it that way, good old scout!

He clucked softly and sorrowfully! "Never s' long as I live, Buck, will I evah fergit th' look that come over his Ma's face. She handed Mister Pomp th' wire — but he didn' hav' his specs, so she had t' read it to him — an' — man — her voice wuz as steady—." Again Charley clucked into his cheek! "Seemed at firs' lak Mister Pomp couldn' understand — then — all of a sudden, seemed lak, h'it come to him. I wuz lookin' t' see th' ol' fellow bust out — but not a single tear com' hoppin' down his face — he warn't th' cryin' kind. Naw — he jus' sorter clutched out f' Mrs. Eddins — clasped her in his arms — sorter like he had

done 'come to attention'— an' wuz listenin' f' sumpthin'. They both jus' stood there an' shivered. I tried
t' say sumpthin' comfortin' like — but th' old man
interrupted me: 'I'm obliged t' you, Charles,' he says,
'f' bringin' th' word — hit's sho' bad news,' he says,
'but,' he says, 'on th' other han',' he says, 'John Yancey
Eddins has won th' highes' an' mos' distinguished
honor that can befall a gallant soldier of our country'."
Charley wiped his greasy fingers on his hunting coat
and turned to me reflectively again. "Do you 'member
whut an' unreconstructed Confed'rate ol' man Pomp
wuz? But in th' end he wuz sold jus' as strong on Uncle
Sam." Charley had the thread of things toward the
knot. "But about that time," he concluded, "ol' man
Pomp raised his face t'odes th' ceilin', an' his whole
heart jus' seem'd t' break out in one great cry — 'Aw
Gawd'— he says —'YOU know,' he says —'h'it ain't
right!' Mrs. Eddins seen he wuz fixin' t' giv' down.
She held him tighter in her arms an' says, soothing like,
'There — there — Daddy,' she says, 'th' Lawd giveth
an' th' Lawd taketh away, blessed be th' name o' th'
Lawd.' Buck, there warn't one single tear ev'ah com'
t' ol' man Pomp's eyes. 'I know,' he wailed; 'I take it
all back — Gawd — but, oh,' he says, 'John Yancey's
th' las' one o' us — no mo' John Yancey — Oh!
Christ,' he says, 'no mo' Eddinses fo' th' wars — no
mo' Eddinses fo' th' wars!' "

—TO AN OLE CULLUD FREN'—

Gumbo an' buckshot, burr haids an' weeds,
Er big dram o' white-mule, is whut I needs.
Saddle up, Jug-mule, ride yo' waves,
Rabbit backbone is whut I craves.

Ram down yo' powder, po' on de shot,
Er noble load whut dis Jug-mule got.
Rabbit houn' yelpin', yawnders mah meat,
Bustin' down de cawn row wid all fo' feet!

Hol' still, Jug-mule, wh'ah mah gun?
Ef de cap-haid busts, I lows t'end his fun.
De Cap'n ain't lookin' an' de dawgs cain't see,
He 'ah go rabbit backbone f' Molly an' me.

Cap'n, thank'ee, dis liquah's jes' rite,
An' dis he 'ah fo' bits meks m' heart all brite,
Me an' yu' bin huntin' sence yu' wuz 'er boy,
He 'ahs yo' ve'y bes' health, suh, an' wishin' yu' joy.

Good night, Cap'n, I'll ten' t' dese mules,
"Git up he'ah now, yu Jug-haided fools."
Coals in de fi'ah place, grease in de pan,
Rabbit in m' belly, an' money in m' han'!

THE NEGLECTED DUCK CALL

An early duck-shooting recollection of mine is of seeing a great many duck calls around but very seldom hearing them blown. Possibly ducks were so plentiful in those days that calls were considered more or less ornamental devices, to be used only in times of abject need, or to furnish sartorial atmosphere "on location."

As I recollect them, the fundamentalist duck hunters of my youth were niftier outdoor dressers than our stereotyped O. D. clan of today. I can visualize some of those old-timers right now. Their duck calls were split-ended affairs, with fancy horn loud speakers. They were worn in a breast pocket or hung from a fancy colored cord knotted about the collars of their London corduroy or velveteen shooting jackets. These latter were cut á la morning affairs of today's semi-formal wardrobe. Hip pocket flasks of today's vintage would have been scorned if lined up beside the leather-bound, capacious receptacles those old sports stowed in the pockets of their tail flaps.

But I can't give their calls much. After a few blows, their reeds either jammed, rattled helplessly and dejectedly out of tune, or else bit one's tongue. How my dear old dad would swear when he yanked out his call, only to find its slotted throat loaded with suffocating tobacco silt or cookie crumbs. It required a world of lung power, unbounded endurance and high optimism to keep them going — much less "tuned up."

Swamp angels and market hunters of that day, however, mothered by a parent necessity, were using handmade calls not much different from today's models. As in most contrivances, our best calls spring from those very models. The most noted of early calls was the "Glodo," made, I think, by a Frenchman famed for his prowess with gun and call on a once well-known southern Illinois marsh. My friend, Guy Ward, of Reelfoot Lake and trap-shooting fame, is the proud possessor of an original Glodo. I have heard that as a reed producer and toner Glodo's experimental turn for metal manipulation was little short of marvelous.

Naturally, different sections of the country have various models of calls. I have seen them embodying fifty forms of trumpets and more acoustic engineering, inside and out. I have seen them made of cane joint, cocobolo, walnut, maple, pine, hard rubber, and with tongues all the way from German silver or copper to thinned down clarinet reeds.

Some of them were good, a lot of them bad, and others indifferent. Their operators were, of course, largely to blame, although kinking and corrosion of reeds account for a majority of call casualties.

As my duck shooting career progressed and the birds became less easy to secure without vocal inducement, I took more interest in duck calls and their possibilities. I bought numerous commercial calls, rebuilt them, cut on, up and down and around them, experimented, and did everything but learn to use them correctly. I made the mistake of trying to perfect the call before I learned how to use it.

I could do fairly well; that is, I didn't make the call sound like "All policemen have big feet." I could tell when I had scared a duck and even had sense enough to realize that ofttimes, my getting in a lot of birds was, for the most part, sheer luck and a good stool of decoys.

I was in the sporting goods business. A friend told me of a pal of his, a great hunter and trapshot, who was transferring to new work in our town. We met shortly, and five minutes after our introduction I knew one thing for sure. And that was, so far as duck calling was concerned, like the chap with the d. t. said to the big-game hunters, "I hadn't seen or heard no calling!"

Holder of mechanical, automotive, electrical and marine engineering licenses, Hooker had applied sound technical training and thought to the production of his call. He threw in, in addition, a lifetime of wildfowling experience that began in a boyhood of market hunting in Iowa and Oklahoma and progressed through all forms of duck shooting in the South and Southwest. Shooting is still the most important part of his life's work. The instant I saw and heard him manipulate a duck call I knew at once that I was listening to a Master of the Art and became at once a pupil.

Now taking lessons in duck calling isn't a bit different from studying the saxophone or banjo. You must want to learn, and you must work. We worked at it in odd moments back in our shipping department. Off behind tiers of deadening crates, we made the rafters ring. I blew my daily dozen, and he responded in his. Note by note, scale by scale, and beat by beat, I strove to master the clear, high hails; the throaty, chuckling feed roll; the shorter, throatier welcome and numerous other duck idioms, maintaining measures of vocal entertainment and out-loud meditation.

By the time our first duck season was over, I received my diploma in the form of a beautifully engraved duck call. But by comparison it was very much like Caruso's telling some light-opera singer that he could do pretty well. After two seasons, however, I began calling well enough to get out on my own hook more or less and become a teacher and critic in the absence of the master.

I have travelled around the duck circuit quite a bit and heard a lot of callers. I have never seen or heard one yet that I consider remotely in the same class with Hooker, and there are undoubtedly any number of great duck callers at large.

Then the World War came along, and Perry Hooker went to England as an aeroplane engine man. He was gone a good while, too. A year and a half later — in January it was — he landed and in four days off the boat was home, wanting a hunt the worst way in the world. There were no ducks in our club; so we took a quail hunt across from there, over beyond the levee, among the cornfields and wild lands along the Mississippi. The river was very high, lipping its banks.

I remember that we found one covey of birds in some tall weeds, right at the water's edge, where the river had backed up and inundated a great area of tall willows under the mainland. At the report of our guns, up from the overflowed tree tops went thousands of ducks, mostly mallards and sprigs. We stared at them in amazement. Following our quail singles, we came to where the willow flats petered out.

A fierce wind was blowing from the north, and after garnering our bob-whites, we stopped and watched flock after flock of ducks, disturbed by our firing, milling in the gale out over the vast expanse of willow tops between us and the white-capped river. Many of them

swept down toward the narrow gap to our end of the
tract, then wheeled and beat it up along the shore line
toward the open end of the willow V. Each of us had
a duck call, not by accident or luck but by second
nature.

We ate a snack, tied up the dogs and told our colored
horse jingler to ride up along the overflow a good piece
and shoot every so often at something, just to keep the
birds stirred. We had no boat, and there were twenty
feet of water off the bank edge. What ducks we could
kill would necessarily have to be either called off over
the mainland or, if dropped into the backwater, left to
be collected next morning with a boat. There was little
danger of any driftage, the tree stems being too matted
for that.

After a bit, a bunch of greenheads came streaking
down the far side of the cut. Hooker opened up. They
wheeled across wind and responded beautifully to the
absolutely perfect call. Half of them, seeking those
unseen birds back in that pocket, circled inland and
beat up-wind through the great bare-branched oaks of
an Indian mound, amid whose undergrowth of cane
and vines we were hiding. He killed four. In fact, we
bagged two limits in the next hour and a half, and only
ten of the fifty fell into the back-water.

Next morning, before daylight, we were again on the
scene, but this time we had a boat with us. At dawn

thousands of ducks rolled and roared out of the vast flat. In a few torrid moments we bagged twelve or fifteen birds, but the sun came up on a clear, warm, windless day, and few, if any, birds ever returned.

We retrieved our left-overs of the day before and went ashore, ruminatively cursing our luck of the weather. No cold, heavy wind to load the backwater with mallards, seeking feed and quiet in its shelter. No. But a fire to boil coffee and eat lunch by, a wagon to haul the boat and ducks home, and two good dogs to find plenty of quail twixt there and the house.

The next season I made a discovery. Maybe duck callers knew or know it, but neither Perry nor I had ever tumbled. And that is, a good duck call like Hooker's is as effective a goose call as you would want if you can and are not afraid to call geese. An offhand but loud blow with a smothering finger that accidently lifted on the proper note brought the tidings. Ensued some heavy practice. And now, by merely blowing just the right volume into our calls and using the same throat stroking, we can send a long goose note a good way. We can triple-tongue the response and gabble too.

By and large, however, the best goose imitators I have ever heard belong, by nature, to certain gifted individuals, whom I envy.

Duck calls and duck calling vary with duck sectors. I have heard guides on one lake make a noise quite unlike any duck I have ever heard. And yet the ducks responded. I'll never forget the shock I experienced in a blind at a ten-dollar-a-day, pay-as-you-enter shooting club on the Illinois River. There were five of us in one blind, with a guide who was a cross between a drill sergeant and a musical director.

We "sports" were lined up in a hide overlooking a poultry-wire pen containing fifty live mallards, feeding on the corn-fed contents of the little pond and scrambling about amid the open water and floating ice blocks in the enclosure. Happening to look down-wind after being assigned my position, I saw a duck beating up toward us. "Yonder comes a duck," I whispered to the sergeant.

He took one look, fell on his knees, closed his nose with thumb and forefinger, and began to yell, "Eenie, eenie, eenie, eenie!" Frankly, I thought he had gone suddenly crazy. But the duck kept steadily on his course and was killed.

Later I learned that this is a common method of calling ducks on the Illinois and, from what I observe, effective enough too. It seems, however, merely a matter of attracting their attention to the open water pens full of live birds. Then, if the ducks are at all inclined to be sociable, they decoy. But I doubt the success of this method of calling in high timber or obscure slashes, with no decoys to back it up.

Another phase of duck calling which interests me is the struggle between the use of decoys and the use of duck calls. In the last fifteen years I have sold thousands of duck calls and many different kinds of decoys. I have belonged to several duck clubs whose memberships comprised over one hundred duck hunters. In one club particularly are men who have been shooting ducks for forty years.

And yet, looking back on it, I do not recall one man among the whole outfit who knows beans about real duck calling. Yet they all have duck calls, but they usually turn these over to their paddlers and depend upon a large supply of birds and a plentiful stool. Hundreds upon hundreds of hunters ignorant of beat, note and tone buy duck and goose calls during the hunting season. This is particularly noticeable to me, as I was just where they are until I took the trouble and practice required to become proficient in the art.

In an article of mine on the use of decoys this statement was made: "In timber woods and pot-hole shooting I would much prefer to have a call and no decoys than decoys and no call." I also stated that the reverse is true on big water and open shooting where sighting of a large stool is the more valuable of the two accessories. I have seen duck hunters — good shots — buy duck calls and produce some of the weirdest squawks imaginable.

A year ago last duck season, a famous sportsman from the East came down to shoot ducks and geese with Perry Hooker and me on the Mississippi. He had used a call some, shooting a great deal out of a blind and sink boxes over big stools, and a rattling good shot he is too. He was at a loss to understand, however, why, in shooting off a big river, we used so few — half a dozen or so — duck decoys. We explained to him that it was because we were shooting in small pot-holes and ponds where decoys would not show until the ducks were close in and that we depended on our calls, adding that in lakes, shallow open ponds and such we used all the stools we could carry.

After listening to Hooker call and actually seeing what such skill could accomplish when pitted single-mouthed, so to speak, against nature, he began to see the light. "Here," he said, "is where I get busy. I've been telling those fellows back home that on big waters a call would help even with big stools, and I have seen what it did with practically no decoys at all. I believe that if I learn to call properly I can get at many a bird up home that would otherwise pass me up."

For the next week, in every spare moment he was to be found sitting opposite Perry down on the river bank, in the tent, or blind, patiently quack-quack-quacking away after an even more patient instructor. Last fall I met him in New York. He wore a broad grin and had his duck call along — one that Hooker had given him. He wanted to blow an exhibition solo in the Ritz. He had, he said, proved his point about the value of a call on any kind of water, with or without decoys, and was ready to hang out his shingle as a duck-calling professor.

The most attractive situation I've ever found for a duck call is in a willow or cypress brake, full of sloughs, pot-holes and pond runways — without decoys. Another beautiful location is at the base of some deep cove off a wide shallow lake, with just a few decoys and an overhead pass flight from which to lure a limit of birds by calling. But give me the tall timber spot. Just my gun, my call and for good measure a fine companionable Chesapeake like old Pat.

There are, of course, some exceptionally excellent commercial calls, and they deserve a better fate than most of them come to. Naturally, however, mass production, shipping, minor details and misuse by oftimes ignorant clerks who don't know the first principles of duck calling render them anything but musical instruments. But one can learn to call with any good product on the market today. They can easily be soaked and adjusted to give good tone.

But the pupil purchaser must have it in his heart to learn. The average untaught duck hunter simply sticks a call into his mouth, draws in a lungful of wind and emits a loud tooting q-u-u-a-a-c-c-k, or rather an attempt at a quack, that results in a glum quonk. He toots and toots, purpling. If he is in a store, the clerk stops him guardedly. If out hunting, incoming highfliers mount higher, and lower prospects take advantage of his brazen charity to detour.

Now watch a caller of the Hooker type. With no bird in sight of his blind, he is constantly advertising for customers. One of his calls, with or without a carrying wind, can be heard for a long, long way. You'll hear the resting call, a well-fed, long-drawnout note — a "Que — Q-U-A-C-K — qua-qua-qua- — ack" running across five or more, usually six quacks, with the accent on the second quack. Then a pause. Then three measured quacks given with well modulated chesty dignity.

Over the cypress may then swing a bunch of four or five mallards who, while yet a long way off, have heard the call and turned. Now a loud welcoming hail, with a rising inflection on the first quack that corresponds to our "W-E-L-L, where th' —— have YOU been?" It runs in three beats, followed immediately by a five beat "Que - quark - quark - quark - quark," repeated rapidly.

Hearing this and, we presume, liking it, our ducks maybe tumble to a lower circling plane. Again the hail; and, if two men are "blinded" together, as Perry and I usually are, one takes up the line or address of welcome where the other leaves off. When our judgment notes sincere interest on the part of the visitors, we begin to offer special inducements, real duck bartering. The loud "Ah-har-har-har—ah-har-har-har" is broken quickly into the muffled chuckling feed roll, sounded by chattering the word "cut" rapidly into the call — "Cut-a-cut-a-cut." By practice you can break it into a "b-u-r-r-ed" vibration by twisting the tongue into an imitation of a quail's buzzing from the grass.

I have read, but strongly dissent, that in blind shooting, once ducks are attracted, it is time to quit calling. That may be all very well on big open water (but I doubt it) over a wide spread of stools where birds can see, hear and come a long way. But Hooker and I have tried it all the ways we know how, and agree that full effectiveness is best obtained by our maintaining the welcome until we drop the calls on to their neck strings and sound off a welcome with our guns.

To most novice duck hunters the call of a duck is a quack. The wood duck may yodel (easily imitated); the sprig may sound his lilting, fluty, twonote quip; the gadwell croak his guttural responses and the teal "tee-hee-tee-ho" its sibilant gyrations — but it is all quack to the novice.

You must study ducks, study tone, and learn to apply their measured tonal characters to individual cases and needs. If possible in your studies, hang around some live decoys at feeding time, early in the morning or about sundown. Try to reproduce with your call their conversational exchanges in quality of tone that blends and sets them off into gladsome refrains. Listen to what they say and how they express it.

But the most delicate adjustment of a call's reed is necessary to successfully maintained tonal reproduction. One kink, and the whole sound changes. If your call jams, don't, if it is an adjustable reed, monkey with it. Blow hard through the other end to loosen possible impedimenta. If there is a kink in the reed, remove it and smooth it evenly, or scrape with a knife blade. But be careful!

Next in importance in learning to call is the use of one's fingers in manipulative muffling or releasing tonal volume. Cup the trumpet end of your call firmly twixt thumb and first finger hollow, curving the other fingers out, close together, to complete the megaphonic extension. Shut down or open the megaphone finger by finger and notice the results. Watch the neophyte caller start the operation. I have seen it a thousand times when selling duck calls to supposed duck hunters — some good shots, too.

The beginner sticks the call's whole end into his mouth — that is, if he knows which end is which — puffs out his cheeks into balloonic proportions, and

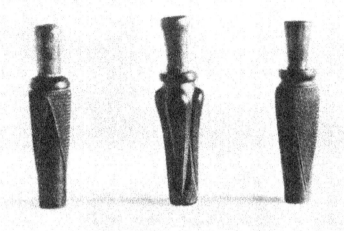

Calls by Tom Turpin, Jo Willingham, and Perry Hooker

The same calls showing their different reeds and slots

turns loose. The finished caller blows over slightly pursed lips — almost you might think, through his teeth. A good call requires about a third of the wind necessary to bring volume from the average call. In the good caller you'll notice, perhaps, a slight vibration of his Adam's apple but that is about all. To throw a far call he elevates the trumpet, but in more intimate passages it is pointed to the water and the finger work carefully choked.

I have seen and tried many first-rate calls — the Harlow, the Beckhart "Big Lake" model, Tom Turpin's new affair, another of cane from Louisiana and others too numerous to recall. To my way of thinking, Hooker's is the most easily blown and best designed I have ever seen or tried. He constructs his sounding box of walnut or clear maple, scraped very thin, to reproduce quality in the amphitheatre, like a cello or violin. Its inset stem is cedar, with the vibration trough very deep and smooth.

His reed, after years of experiment which led him through many alloys and pures, is now a masterpiece of rustless Monel metal. He works these reeds down to a form and thickness all his own. They are hand scraped, and all his calls are tuned out in the open and across water. This is no advertisement, because any good duck caller with a mechanical turn can do the same thing. Could you get a Hooker call? Possibly so, if he likes you and has the time to make one and present you with it. If he ever should, you're to be congratulated for having come into possession of a "Strad" among duck calls.

Another beautiful call with which Hooker has experimented with considerable degree of success has a sounding rod and box case practically identical with his Monel metal call. The reed of his other call, however, is made from smoothed-down hard rubber. In size — that is, width, length and curve — it is a duplicate of the Monel metal reed. The floor, or trap-lines, of the sounding box of Monel metal call has, to accommodate the flippant metal, a curved surface.

His hard rubber reed, however, has to lie on an absolutely straight sounding cover. In other words, the two reeds are not interchangeable. Working down the hard rubber reed is a task, as it has to slope from about $64/1000$ down to practically nothing at the far end. Even then, the work has to be done individually on each reed with a piece of sandpaper, and then each call is blown at intervals as the reed is smoothed down to take the fullest measure of initial energy and tone.

Duck calling has no significance of sex appeal, as has turkey calling during the "gobble" or moose calling in the rut. There is nothing unsportsmanlike about it, far less than in baiting pond holes and blotting out twenty yard masses over pens full of live decoys.

Then give me a good call, my big gun, a sand-bar hole or a tule hide — and you may have the rest. Upon the aftermath of such days hang "all the laws and the prophets" of duck shooting. By learning to call you will have gauged an added thrill of accomplishment that will prove an enduring comrade and a pal in need in your blind.

AFTERWORD

Since writing the above (1928) I am glad to say it did its bit and served a purpose in stimulating the national use of duck calls. Within two seasons following publication of "The Neglected Duck Call," I received just short of five hundred letters from men wanting Hooker model calls. Goodness only knows how many poor Perry Hooker had, for finally it became necessary for him to mail a 'form letter' to applicants saying he didn't furnish them commercially.

But the art, meanwhile, had taken deeper root elsewhere. I doubt if the "Turkey Caller's Clan" has ever known a more skillful student, artisan or artist than my good old friend and thoroughgoing sportsman, Tom Turpin. Tom, a contractor and master home builder, with a flair for the scroll saw, calipers, and sandpaper, also possesses an as yet unsatisfied yen for "gobbler gittin'" with a three barrel or rifle, 'scope mounted. His magazine articles on turkey calls and turkey hunting, are voluminous.

[167]

Around my old sporting goods store, Tom Turpin was always welcome and instructive company. It was there, incidentally, he met Perry Hooker and became intrigued with the possibilities of duck calls from the gunning, artistic, and commercial standpoint. Tom Turpin never does anything half way. Months merged into years of experiment. My work took me away from our home town, and, for several years I barely sighted Tom. But I knew from an occasional letter and magazine advertising that he had his "calls" on the market and was also putting out phonograph records of them for instruction in the hunter's art.

Last Fall (1932) it was my good fortune to find myself in company with Tom Turpin, as quail shooting guests of Mr. Robert M. Carrier at his marvellous "Bob White" preserve "Barnacre Lodge" several miles west of Sardis, Panola County, Mississippi. Our host was also helping entertain a sportsmen's meeting held down in the "Big Woods" just prior to opening of their big game shooting season. So, Tom Turpin had brought along a "gripsack" full of duck, crow, and turkey calls, for the edification of some seventy-five fine fellows.

I honestly believe that Tom Turpin's demonstration of his various game calls, is the greatest "outdoor act" of such circles, on or off the boards of vaudeville. And its most admirable feature is that he hasn't the faintest idea (until he reads this maybe) just how clever it is. As Tom humorously puts it in opening the show: "The duck, crow or turkey call in the hands of the unschool-ed, is the nation's greatest Conservation asset."

That night we had a long talk. Tom Turpin has reproduced the celebrated old Reelfoot "Glodo model" duck call, and has and is, experimenting with all sorts of woods, reed metals, and sound passages. Wherever he has heard of a "master" duck caller, he has gone to that individual and put his paces on a phonograph record.

"Buck," said Tom, that evening, as I pocketed with glee and thanks a gift in the form of a long range duck call fashioned from bakelite, "I've gone from Iowa to Louisiana; from Reelfoot to the Arkansas ricefields and pin-oaked timber flats and up through the Illinois river regions. Each sector usually has its individual duck calling champ. And some of them are good. But a thing I've never heard in all my travels is some one fellow who can 'blow' all the different 'duck lan-guages' of the circuit. The Reelfoot guide sounding his 'High-ball' or 'Paducah' call across big water, would scare the daylights out of ducks in the timber. And the Louisiana 'Cajan,' twittering away with his throaty little cane instrument and filed rubber reed would draw a smile from the 'feed call and chuckler' of the cypress brakes. But, properly applied to localized needs, they are effective. I've listened to many a one, and I agree with you that Hooker is a real 'champ'."

"But Tom," I interrupted, "as a matter of fact, after listening to your performance tonight, I'm prepared to say that I have met a man who can really 'blow 'em all'."

"Oh!" rejoined my old friend, modestly, "I know 'em all, naturally, but that doesn't mean I can beat the world, by a darn sight."

"Tom," I queried, "have you ever read what Roark Bradford's negro character, John Henry, replied in connection with any question as to his spike driving ability? Well, that's how I feel about your duck calling. John Henry says, in effect: "I'se John Henry, from th' Black River country whar' th' sun don't never shine — I ain't de bes' spike driver in de worl', but de man whut was, is dead — an' dat don't leave nobody but me."

THOU AND THY GUN BEARER

I HAVE never hunted in Africa, where gun bearers of the safari type do service; negroes upon whose nerve and coolness in time of acute danger depends life. But being Southern-born and practically raised afield, it has been my happy lot to come in contact with full many a darky hunter. Over such a period, one of well-nigh forty years, I call to mind several specimens of the Afro-woodsman offshoot whose staunch help and teachings have had much to do with my later successful traverse of the outdoorman's domain. But the kind I knew has pretty nearly passed; his pioneer negative has faded in the glare of modernity. But I know that on my native heath and in my land there are many men who realize the fibre of the breed I mean. He was the darky who loved the hunt with all the innate under-standing of his jungle forebears and brought to it the intelligent zest of his master. He played a humble second fiddle in all save toil and glad acclaim in the spoils of the chase. He knew the silent paths and stillest corners of the big timber; the swamp crossings and bayou tracings were open books. "Varmint" haunts and the lore of graveyard rabbits came as second nature, and the cult of "yarbs" and influence of the moon upon planting and biting fish required but a turning of nature's pages. Winds whispered to him certain mysterious meanings; he foretold the fates by virtue of cloud linings and prophecy of the rainbow. He lived in the very lap of season! Who knew the covey grounds as well as he; who skulked a squirrel woods with as flittering and shadowy patience; who took more certain toll from turkey roosts that yielded victims with the mingling of moon flight and dawn? Flight lines and goose-tracked sandbars knew no more adept hound, while his traps and dead-falls outmatched the denizens of a region where footprints told no tales! And he knew all these things in his own particular way; which means that his understanding was past our own and subject only to his own pleasure and friendship for the imparting thereof. This was the darky who served because he knew faith and honor, who knew his place and knew that the white man knew he knew it, and by that signal and mutual recognition found confidence and fulness of purpose and co-operation. To him no road was too long if duty called. He fetched and carried and bore heavy burdens willingly, read his Bible diligently and frowned upon the tendencies of an encroaching generation. When he accompanied his "whitefolks" afield there was companionship without intimacy, comradeship in common purpose and full realization of appreciation on both sides. But alas! with the coming of civilization we find them now retreating from the trenches of service into more peaceful billets of reminiscence. An old log-hewn cabin far beyond the "new-ground," a comfortable rocking-chair outside in the shade of summer and a warm fireside in winter— and a pipe always! The incidents I recall here I mean simply enough as a tribute to a faithful friend who taught me much and did for me that which was best in his conception of the theory of life and unselfish service!

Such was "Uncle" Phil Gwynne, clubhouse keeper, cook, paddler-in-chief and general all-around generalissimo of our duck club Waponoca. 'Way back in the early eighties, when the club was organized from a shelter tent into a log cabin and thence into a small white cottage, Uncle Phil was unanimously put in charge. He knew intimately and personally all the gentlemen who comprised the limited membership of that day, by virtue of having waited on poker games, served at banquets, cooked on deer hunts and played around generally with most of them for many years. Uncle Phil had been born a slave, was proud of it, cast in his lot with the Confederacy and lived and died an

ardent and argumentative Democrat. Given three toddies of any of his gentlemen friends' good liquor, Uncle
Phil could produce the most enthralling rhapsody con-
cerning the benefits of democracy that any political
organ ever breathed o'er Eden as accompaniment. He
had personally danced attendance upon practically
every Confederate general of any note, and been
present at every "who's-who" battle of the late un-
pleasantness, to hear him tell it, and although at times
a variance of dates claimed his presence at two battles
at the same time, he was never at a loss and supplied
details of so colorful a nature in the interim that his
audience overlooked mere trifles of a few years.

But at heart and soul Uncle Phil was a thoroughgoing sportsman and an admirer of every gentleman
who knew and owned a good gun or dog. No pot-metal
guns or low-blooded bird dogs for Uncle Phil! He
owned an old ten-gauge Westley Richards himself, and
called all the fine dogs of his patrons his own. Yet
with it all no humbler soul ever saw sunrise; no kindlier
spirit ever sought firm ground for its circle of friends.
When I first knew Uncle Phil I was a mere lisping
shaver just graduating from "kilties" to "pants." Even
then he had given up hard paddling and exposure and
taken over the clubhouse and cooking end of the game.
Occasionally, if a shortage of pushers occurred or he
wished to convey an especial privilege, Uncle Phil

went on the lake—and when he did it was always a memorable day for the lucky one. He was a natural born hunter, a keen shot, and quite the best marker-down of cripples I have ever seen. I have seen him out with Daddy and Mister Arthur and Baltimore, his huge Chesapeake Bay dog, when the flight was intense, the mud and rushes deep and thick, and excitement at its height. Sometimes there would be three or four ducks down or falling. Yet Uncle Phil was never at a loss. He went overboard to one side and Baltimore another, and before long the pair would come slushing and mushing back, and Baltimore was hardly ever more than "one up" on the old chief.

Uncle Phil's education, gleaned from the contact of a lifetime with quality "whitefolks," was far beyond the average of his race at that time, and he put it to good use. By religion he was a devout Methodist and in a log church which his "flock" has erected on a nearby Indian mound his faith and goodness shone forth in service that involved preaching, ministering to the sick and teaching Sunday school. When Christmas time rolled around Uncle Phil visited the city and carried back with him enough good cheer to make a real Yuletide for his colored folks. But it was, after all, Uncle Phil's kitchen that held for me a magnetic attractiveness. His culinary domain was housed in a commodious quarter aft, connected with the clubhouse by a covered gangway off which was set the game and paddlers' plunder room. It was my custom, upon return from shooting, to ease quietly into Uncle Phil's place of business and from the vantage point of a seat upon an empty shell box, set well aside from channels of traffic, amid pots and barrels and crocks, to listen to the old fellow's discourse upon hunting, cooking, the theory of the universe or a tolerant discourse upon the rise and fall of the Roman, black, yellow, or Caucasian empire.

There was a wide, open fireplace and chimney corner, a region pendant with soot-covered rods and hooks, and gratings turning brick red in the heat of glowing coals, while from a big range came bubblings and rumblings as covered pots and stewpans gave vent to pent-up emotions of cookery. Hams hung from the rafters and there was invariably at the evening hour a comforting odor of hot, browning biscuits and coffee that at times brought one to a condition bordering upon mutiny against patience. And all the while Uncle Phil pottered in and out, his two sprigs of gray twisted forelock and aristocratic "goatee" giving him a weird shadow upon the curtains. He peeked into a pot here, poked a sinister but ministering fork there, opened the oven and prodded a pie or scanned a batch of biscuits or corn muffins—and talked all the time. At such periods the old man's fancy naturally enough ran to food. In slave days and after, for he was an old man even then,

he had been a steamboat cook on the palatial liners that
ran from Memphis to New Orleans. He had cooked in
private kitchens of Louisiana aristocrats. And many of
our club members had taken him with them to the
Dakota prairies and sloughs when they went for
chicken shooting. He knew each member's fads and
fancies in the way of food and service. While I sat on
my shell box and elicited talk by an occasional inquiry,
Uncle Phil would run riot on his cooking prowess.

At such times, then, Uncle Phil harked back to brave
steamboat and New Orleans days. He babbled of eggs
"Coquelin" and oysters "Rockafellar," of snipe broiled whole as M'sieu Gaston himself had taught him
amid frightful admonitions in event of failure in the
matter of a certain daring and piquante sauce.

There was catfish court bouillon, with crab omelette
and mushroom dressing; demi-lyonnaise potatoes and
smoking drip coffee. Thence flights of gastronomic
revery winged toward gumbo and red snappers, the
latter baked in fine herbs, with panfish or sheepshead
done in versatile measures of excellence. There were
roasted fat mallards from some rice marsh; teals, gar-
landed with oysters tucked up with bacon strips and
broiled into a buttery state of utter deliciousness. He
conjured gnawing pictures of game stew, a lowly *poule
d'eau*, for instance, shriven into a marvel of appetite by
a mere turn of curry, tomato and rice, garlic and a pot-

[177]

pourri of secret ingredients. Thence Uncle Phil trailed off into courses of upland yield, while I, knees drawn to chin and mouth adrool, listened while he prated of smothered quail and roast prairie chicken, with spring lamb on the side, when available for a feast—a mere babe, of say, thirty pounds, roasted as only such a morsel offering should be, with delicate baste and mint extract timed to the second.

Followed crappies and bass, fried de luxe out of doors, in a delirium of sputtering fats and fancies, with corn pone and coffee on the side and potato chunks browned to taste and served with drawn butter over all. Entered tender young squirrels, with a rich tang from mulberry feasting, hips padded with pork slivers, with just a dash of tabasco and done rare over hickory coals. There were tales of venison, stalked and slain by one Maspero and roasted in the ground as to ribs and chops and balanced into sausage with "shoate" shavings, pepper, "yarbs" and a faint soupçon of rare old wine. Flanking these came roasting ears, butter-oiled and fumed under oak shavings; new potatoes and bales of limp, succulent asparagus. Or, if Uncle Phil's fancy fell upon a course dinner, his musings ran the gamut of anchovies and oyster cocktails on down to orange brulait. But when he reached barbecue and stuffed beef heart and a pan dish of sweet potato and tomato bread balls and squirrel dumpling all mixed up and browned over the top, the voice of appetite crashed into a crescendo of demand, and I usually fell from my shell box and ran beyond the lure of his voice; or else, taking advantage of Uncle Phil's turned back, yielded to temptation and robbed the nearest pan. I can taste those stolen tid-bits yet, they still set my mouth a-watering.

A memorable occasion brought us to the club one time just after I had strained at the bonds of youth until given a gun of my own, and Daddy, not wishing to be bothered with me or bother the others, left me in charge of Uncle Phil. There was considerable bantering and betting in the crowd as to who'd be high gun that evening. During the forenoon I hunted the cypress brakes around the clubhouse and amassed a bag total of four squirrels and a "flicker," and after lunch cast about for a try at some more worthy quarry. About mid-afternoon Uncle Phil whistled up Baltimore, told me to get my gun and shells and we piled into his private bateau. My delight knew no bounds. We paddled silently up the mile or more of narrow creek that drained from the lakes. It was a glorious late November afternoon, when the warmth of midday had just begun to tingle with the crisp approach of impending frost, and the sun filtered comfortably down through the interlacing cypress giants that overhung the bayou. From Little Lake we heard two or three guns at work, and as we approached its entrance we heard from up on Big Lake the deep roaring "B-o-o-m" of the black powder of that day.

Uncle Phil ran the bateau ashore just before we reached the spread of water, and led me across a waste of spongy willow flat to a mud slough cast away from sight behind a wall of cypress timber. At the water's edge a gigantic stump offered a wonderful hide, and I could tell by its warm, sawdusty interior that this was a much-used and favorite haunt of Uncle Phil's. We made ourselves comfortable, Baltimore curled up at Uncle Phil's feet, and that worthy, after lighting his pipe, lapsed into quiet drowsing. Not a duck in sight! But the roar of guns on the lakes continued and I grew restless and denounced my guide's choice of a blind. The old man awoke, listened to my say, smiled knowingly —"Jus' you wait, l'il Boss; dey'll be he'ah!" Then, in the midst of a soothing yarn as to what he did when the Yankees were on the point of blowing up the *Queen-of-the-West*, there came from overhead the whistling banter of many wings, and into that mud puddle sifted a great swarm of clustering mallards. Down we crouched, and I can see the eager strain in Baltimore's yellow eyes as he realized that his afternoon's fun, too, had begun. To check my movement of preparedness, Uncle Phil seized me by the shoulder and pressed me down. "Hol' still, l'il Boss, hol' still — mo' comin'!" And how they did circle and chuckle

[180]

and flutter down into that loblolly hole! The very air seethed with applicants for space.

As though it were yesterday, I can still hear my black mentor's word to fire — he with his ten-gauge bellowing and I with my twelve-gauge hammering. How those ducks did pile out of there when that dose of shot raked them on the water and again as they rose! It was unsportsmanlike, but it was business to Uncle Phil and me, for the old rascal had a purpose in taking me out that afternoon. I dashed from the blind and all but dove into the soupy pond, with Baltimore ahead of me and surging to business among the slain! Uncle Phil cut a long pole and with this as a rake and much adventure in the mud and Baltimore's aid we at length retrieved the kill. Twenty-nine magnificent mallards —— I blush now, but I swelled with pride at the time! Piling them into bunches of five and hiding them out, we renewed our policy of watchful waiting. I was now a thorough convert to Uncle Phil's method of acquiring game and joyfully proclaimed our joint prowess. After a little while another swarm of birds dropped in, and again we made a red afternoon with them. Then, as the afternoon waned, they came in pairs and smaller gangs, and I banged away to my heart's content, while Uncle Phil alternately bowled over a greenhead and instructed me as to distance and lead. At length, when the sun had left us but a cold rim through the cypress, Uncle Phil eyed his huge silver watch and began transporting our bag to the bateau. "Time t'git home and start gittin' supper!"

The limit was fifty ducks and by count we had fifty-nine, so Uncle Phil appropriated the extra nine for table use, and hung my bunch of fifty handsome birds in the game room. When the grown-ups arrived there I was, apparently unconcerned and trying to appear at ease at their wondering queries; but I fear there was no small amount of unconscious swank — and I know that I asked odds of no monarch—that night.

My first wild turkey! The New Year's Day when Daddy and I and a pusher—old Fred—tipped over an ice-coated bateau up in Little Lake and sank ingloriously into two feet of water so cold it fairly burnt. But we paddled like mad down the creek to the clubhouse, and what with having kept circulation going and a warm fireside and a rub-down with dry clothing, we emerged none the worse. Daddy said that in so far as he was personally concerned he was willing to call it a day—and did. But none o' that for Youth! Uncle Phil donned his gum boots, took down the ten-gauge and 'lowed that he and l'il Boss would go down the creek a ways and see what they could "scar' up!" Save for a narrow strip of channel, the bayou was frozen and a four-inch snow had us well put to it to thread the jungle. We were standing just outside the wall of a

giant canebrake, debating a shot at some mallards flying the open water, when some distance below us a
drove of great, clumsy-looking birds rose from the
timber opposite and sailed across to our side.

"Dar, now!" muttered Uncle Phil, turning hurried-
ly into the cane. "Come on, l'il Boss, les' head 'em off!"

"What are they, Uncle Phil—buzzards?"

"Turkey!" he threw back over his shoulder and split
the bush. We ran until I fairly gasped for breath. Suddenly at the foot of a huge oak just off a clearing in the
underbrush, Uncle Phil sank to his knees and drew
forth a bit of whitened bone. He was going to "call,"
and an instant later the quaint yelp sounded through
the snow-clad woods. "Dey most likely won't, but dey
may," he muttered. But in just a moment, it seemed,
with a great flapping of wings a giant bird rose some
distance off and came sailing directly over us. I saw
him coming and it seemed to me that with cold fingers
the drawing of my hammer seemed hopeless. But
somehow I got them back and with a prayer in my boy's
heart I swung the tubes out past that mottled head until
I lost it and pulled off both barrels. As in a dream I saw
the turkey waver and come swirling down. But when
he hit the snow he lit running and then ensued a race
that laid Uncle Phil, shouting with laughter, against
a tree root. A winged racehorse of a wild turkey hot-
footing it for life, with a frenzied, rapid-fire fat boy

in hot pursuit. Uncle Phil told Daddy afterward that the turkey and I tore a right-of-way through the woods big enough for a steamboat; but, be that as it may, I know that at the moment when I was about played out Mister Gobbler became entangled in a vine. And there, between puffs and pants, I stood at ease until my wind came back, and then with malice and aforethought I shot that bird soundly dead—and bore him back in triumph. A fine gobbler he was, too, with a beard that was worth keeping and wattles that set off the bronze of him to perfection. What a day that was! We lost all sense of time and direction for a while, for Uncle Phil's blood was up and he set to work with a will. Three more fat birds fell into his vocal snare and we took turns laying them low. It was nigh sundown when we circled out of the timber and made it across the fields to the clubhouse. We had four turkeys, had seen deer tracks, and I am sure that a trade of jobs with the Czar of all the Russians would have been a paltry offer to me that night.

Years later, years that multiplied with adventures as the trail led on and on, Uncle Phil began to fade. He pottered cheerfully about and never complained—but he knew! One of his grandchildren came to aid him in the kitchen and he still talked to me evenings. But his old ten-gauge hung idle from its antler'd rack, and his hunting days were always to be—tomorrow. Good old soul! He still crawled painfully to church meetings occasionally and Christmas was always made an event long to be remembered for him. But finally there came a day when the best thing Uncle Phil could do was to smile a wan smile from his bed — and rest there. We all sensed that now he was slipping fast. How well I remember his last night, for I was over there with Daddy and Mister Arthur and several other members who cherished the old slave. For hadn't they been together when storms beat upon them; when suns rose o'er the stubble of the northlands and set for them in the dark undergrowth of Southern canebrakes? Hadn't they known together all the joys of the chase and found therein for one another only boon comradeship and respect? We sat around the yawning fireplace that bitter-cold night, each one for the most part busy with thoughts of sadness for the quaint old soul so near the verge. At length, Mister Arthur and Daddy, unable to stand it longer, slipped quietly away and went across the pasture lot to Uncle Phil's cabin. And I, unnoticed, trudged along behind them—I wanted to see Uncle Phil, too.

A dim light burned in the room where the old man lay, and, as in most darky homes when the final hour impends, a group of friends and relatives and kindred offspring had gathered, standing and sitting about in various postures of dejected waiting. We tiptoed to the bedside and stood looking down at the pathetic figure, lying there so frail and still. Child that I was, his likeness in the fullness of manhood came sweeping across the years. I saw him tall and vigorous, scarce bending under the weight of a deer, or outlined a black statue as he stood to pole the duck boat into the very teeth of a wintry gale. I saw him again as he peeked and pried into the pots and pans and cast his shadow upon the kitchen curtains! Mister Arthur bent down and spoke very gently—"Uncle Phil—this is Mister Arthur—how do you feel—do you know me?" The drooping eyelids fluttered and for a moment the old man's eyes searched Mister Arthur's face without understanding, and then just the drift of a smile repaid the understanding that his treasured friend had come to him in this hour! And then he whispered—"Th' mud is deep, suh, I'se holdin' onto de willers but I'se sinkin' fas'!" Mister Arthur placed his hand upon Uncle Phil's and I believe that as the white hand clasped the black one there passed between those two old friends a message that they alone understood—and perhaps from that hour looked forward to! Silently Daddy and I stepped forward and petted Uncle Phil's hand, and each time the eyelids fluttered feebly. He had seen us—and understood—I know! Then we went quietly again, out into the night. Ah! Surely it was an evening—a noble evening for the soul of a tired but true old hunter to

fare forth alone upon the long, mystery trail. For a
wind had risen, a near gale from the south that sent
cloud platoons scurrying northward and yet somehow
beat upon us with a touch of warmth in its breath. It
meant, that breath, that ere daybreak the ice would
boom and crack and show great lanes of black open
water and that upon the heels of the blow a rain would
scour the glazed remnant and send the first challenge
of spring into the sloughs. And with it the premier
voyageurs of a winged host would spiral from the
broad bosom of the lake and send their flight lanes
toward northern climes. Sunrise would flash upon the
brilliant plumage of transient sprigtails and bands of
fickle teal would dart about the favorite blinds that
Uncle Phil had built and loved so well.

From the cabin behind us—where a light still
gleamed faintly—came a low, minor wail that mounted as a chorus of blending voices wound their chords
into a death chant. We halted and Mister Arthur and
Daddy stood with bowed heads.

"We were just in time, Arthur," said Daddy.
"Uncle Phil has gone!"

"Yes, Miles," replied Mister Arthur, and his voice
trembled just a bit; "Uncle Phil is with Bun and
George and Robert and all the old boys of ours in the
Happy Hunting Grounds—Heaven grant him a good
flight and God rest his good old soul!"

THE FAMILY HONOR

Pat, for short of the stud book's pompous tally, was one from a litter of six Chesapeake Bay puppies whelped of noble sire and dauntless dam. Bred in the purple and fearless, intelligent water dogs, Pat's old folks, Count and Beck, dared conditions that any day could produce to balk their line of business duty. Acknowledged king and queen of their respective territories; he on his side of the Potomac — she on hers. Duck gunners had long since been wont to seek hungrily and bid high for their progeny. More than once, after some particularly brilliant retrieve, old Beck had heard Marse Henry offered all kinds of real money for her. But Beck had quit worrying. When such "cracks" were pulled, Marse Henry's eyes twinkled as he knocked the ashes out of his pipe, just to prolong the suspense of negotiation. Clearing his throat by way of possibly appearing even more interested, he'd drawl: "Have you got as much as five hundred bucks to lay on the barrel head for a sure enough Chesapeake?" "Yep," more than one wildfowler had shot back at him; "I've got all of that for the like of her!" "Fine," Marse Henry would assent, restuffing his smoke-screener; "in that case you jus' keep on savin' up an' when you've got a thousand or so to go on top of that five hundred — why — why — even then I doubt if it would do any good to take another wallop at me. Why, hell's bells! five grand or a stack of greenbacks high as the Washington monument for this old sister wouldn't interest me in the least." And knowing Henry, they knew he meant just that, foolish and sentimental as it seemed or sounded.

But Marse Henry, good friend and neighbor that he is, rarely, if ever, sold a pup. He made a present here and there, until, out of Beck's last presentation, only little sister Pat and big brother Fritz remained. Doc had had first pick, but I'm coming to that later. Somehow, first one and then another of her babies "turned up missing." Drifted away mysteriously while Beck was out foraging. Those last two, Fritz and Pat, grew increasingly precious. What a mother! How she petted and loved and licked them. And with what ominous ferocity she guarded them, too! A grand specimen of the breed, old Beck. A great sway-backed, wavy-withered, lemon-eyed creature; massively compact and rugged. Lying there amid sun patches filtering through Marse Henry's apple orchard, she tenderly dreamed

"I know my job!"

Fritz and Pat retrieving canvasbacks

away her youngster's puppyhood. Hard to tell apart, those two brown, furry balls; rolling, leaping and snarling in rough dispute for possession of the long suffering house kitten. Beck's misty, blinky eyes wandered from her darlings — along the Maryland heights and far across the lordly Potomac toward Virginia and Mount Vernon. What were her thoughts? Your guess is as good as mine. Of canvasbacks, blackheads, or whistlers slithering into Marse Henry's decoys? Or that terrible day she broke through sharp skim-ice offshore and was trapped in a floe? She had cut her forelegs to ribbons crashing shoreward for her life. A close call, that! But she had delivered the goods, a mere "trash duck," at that. No, Beck and death weren't entire strangers. But stuff like that was all water gone under the bridge — all in her day's work. When their times came, she didn't want Pat or Fritz "showing yellow," either. Anything but that. Happy all her days long, Becky. No dog on earth could ever have had as kindly a master, or a happier home. Dog heaven, that farm! All and more than one wanted, to eat — and such grub! Marse Henry to hunt crows with and pitch driftwood for her and the babies to retrieve. And plenty of rabbits to jump and chase through the corn and pasture. If all that was in Beck's mind, she had a great deal to be thankful for, but she gave value received and a golden disposition. Maybe, just about then, she was thinking of how Fritz and Pat happened into this jolly old duck shooting world.

Last New Year's day — of all times! For quite a while Beck and the farmhold had been looking forward to a "blessed canine event." Marse Henry had been overly solicitous of her lately. Beck had noticed him looking at her counting on his fingers. On several occasions he had quietly latched the kennel and slipped off down to the blind without her. And maybe she hadn't howled. The Colonel had to come and tell her to hush, and ask if she wasn't ashamed of herself making all that fuss. Then he'd grin and given her a piece of sweet corn-pone. Good old girl!

That particular New Year's morning had fetched in a keen, northwest blow, a regular rip-snorter that had been brewing all night. Beck heard it moaning and then roaring around the snug dog house. She knew there'd be drift ice in the river, and a nasty chop for any dog to buck. When Marse Henry and Doc stalked through the yard snapping their flashlights and adjusting packs, Beck tumbled out, flourished about and made it plain that she expected to punch the clock as a matter of course. But Marse Henry said: "No, no, old folks, not today — the hay for yours. 'Doc' prescribes rest and quiet!" Then he collared her and patted and joked her back into the shed; thinking, too, he'd snapped down the door-catch on his way out. But duck hunters have a way of hurrying, with daylight in the offing. After a bit, when howling hadn't prevailed and restlessness wouldn't slack, Beck suddenly shoved hard against the door — and it swung open. The outer gate was a tight squeeze, but she made it. It was easy, then, to track her men down the river road. She caught up just as they deposited their plunder outside the shack. That was Beck's first "break."

"Well, I'll jus' be — looka' here, 'Doc'," Marse Henry cussed, trying to frown at her as she waddled up to them; "if here ain't old Beck — why — why — I locked that door — how th' ——, you gotta' go home — this ain't any way to run a duck hunt — you ain't got any business foolin' aroun' this river a day like today." Beck sensed this meant business. Marse Henry was sputtering sore. The situation called for a number of tail wags to get in close enough to roll over and do a "beg." "Heck of a note," chuttered Marse Henry, only he didn't say "heck;" "it'll take half an hour to lead her back up yonder — darn near daylight — and we can't tie her here on this cold bank." Then Doc made a suggestion, and old Beck got her second "break." "Henry," said Doc, "I'll tell you what — let's take her on out to the blind — it's warm, and comfortable and she can lie there just as safely as she would in the kennel — anyway — there's a day left — isn't there?" It was coming light with a rush, and Marse

Henry weakened. He had bent to rub Beck behind her ears, so she snuggled up closer and gave him a paw-poke. That settled it. "Well," agreed Marse Henry, "all right, but she musn't do a lick of work!" The blind, that winter, was staked fifty yards offshore. Ira, the handy-man, was just skiffing in from anchoring the decoys. A hundred or more black, bobbing specks were swinging with the tide. With much ado as to Beck's comfort, all hands loaded in and Ira effected an easy transfer. Marse Henry lit an oil stove in one end of the hooded blind, and made Beck curl up in some warm straw and sacks, at the other. Ira paddled ashore while Marse Henry and Doc shoved shells into their heavy double guns, tobacco'd their "dudeens" and made ready to operate on any early arrivals. Marse Henry, suddenly remembering something, had just picked up a chain and turned toward Beck's end when Dock hissed —"Henry — Henry — mark left — down — quick!"

Marse Henry ducked, and grabbed for his gun. There was a second or two's quivering ecstasy that is prelude to man's symphony of sport — then — Pop — pop — poppity — pop! A chain rattled on the floor! After all, it was instinct and business pride, with Beck. The family honor must be upheld. She just had to go, and that was all there was to it. Up in a flash; a headlong plunge past Marse Henry's rubber booted shins — and a leaping dive off the outside splash step.

[194]

Sheer, teeth-gritting nerve carrying her and a precious burden through an icy surge. More than she had bargained for, at that. She realized it, pretty quick, too. But, somewhere out there — somewhere out there — puff-puff — cripples might be getting away. That was her business, cripples and dead 'uns. Things would just have to take care of themselves — she'd see them through. She had heard but lost Marse Henry's swearing and bawling — "Come back he'ah, you ole fool!" But just then she'd topped a swell, sighted a still struggling canvasback, and flung herself toward it through crest smother. Three such trips she ploughed, at each return successfully eluding Marse Henry's frantic efforts to snatch her collar and haul her into the hide. Really, she was about "all in," and glad to climb in with the last victim. She was panting heavily and had a draggy feeling.

Never had she seen or heard Marse Henry take on so; swearing to himself and wishing to this, that and the other he had herded her back to the kennel in the first place. Half the time she couldn't tell whether he was "cussin' or cryin'!" He and Doc made all manner of palaver over her after she slunk into the straw. Doc dried her off with an old piece of quilt, and Marse Henry moved the heater closer. She remembered dropping into a doze. Up on the shooter's bench something was said about "the greatest exhibition of instinct!"

Doc was doing most of the talking. Marse Henry was still cussing himself. Shortly thereafter, or at any rate during a later bombardment, Marse Henry and Doc in the act of a hurried reload, caught two or three faint whimpers from old Beck's corner and some scuffling about in the hay. Having, at one time or another, become familiar with such sounds, they gazed at each other in amazed incredulity. Then Doc dove for a hurried preliminary examination. And Doc knows his dogs, too. "Get busy, Doc, this is your first case of the year," grinned Henry, standing around first on one foot and then the other, while cans and blackheads whisked by unheeded. Doc announced, after awhile, that mother and children were doing as well as could be expected. Meanwhile Ira had brought the boat, and Marse Henry sent him to the house for a flannel lined basket and the car. The shoot went A.W.O.L. for awhile and there was reunion and celebration at the house. Marse Henry chuckled as he and Doc lugged their afternoon's bag up the road, at nightfall. "Those sure ought to be great dogs — born right there in the duck blind — what do you know about THAT — if they haven't got everything a water-dog needs, then there's no such thing as pre-natal influence." To which Doc made answer, taking cover with small loss of professional dignity, "not all of us agree, Henry, that there is any such thing — however — I — er — ahem

— am — er — inclined to believe — er — that — er
— this particular case may prove a light-shedding and
strengthening factor in affirmative observation!"
"Well," came back Marse Henry, "all that you're
talking about may be so, but be that as it may, in view
of medical services rendered, your general all around
participation and the happy termination of this salu-
brious occasion, you get first litter pick — that's fair,
ain't it?" And maybe Doc didn't grab while the choosing was good and old Beck in a consenting frame of
friendship.

Well, perhaps some such memories flitted through
her mind as she lay under the apple trees that afternoon, watching Patsy and Fritz devil the kitty.

Autumn was in the very air. Hillsides flamed and
russet girdles wove in and out among coniferous headlands. Came cool days when Marse Henry, meeting
me on the street, cocked an eye aloft and allowed —
"Boy, there's that ole feelin' in th' vicinity o' my mind
sorter like ducks — how 'bout you?" I'd admit it, and
find myself unconsciously but hopefully following
Marse Henry's slant skyward for a chance glimpse of
early migrants. You never can tell about ducks. Then
we'd talk ducks awhile longer and branch off onto
guns and loads. That particular day, however, Marse
Henry had said —"I guess you'll be headin' south,

yourself, before long — mos' any day now?" He
opened the old pipe's throttle, a sure sign of some
truly deep stuff! "How'd you like to take Pat down
south where ducks and geese are so plentiful — and —
and — sorter start breakin' her for me?"

There is the glimmer of burnished sacrifice in such
friendship. Men have climbed the Golden Stairs for
less than that. But temptation! Take Pat away from
Marse Henry and the Colonel, and old Beck? What if
something happened to her? It was up to me to hesi-
tate, but I lost. The former joys of breaking my own
great dogs, gone these several seasons — and now —
opportunity to train a grand ten month's beauty for
Marse Henry. It was just too good to be true. Two
weeks later, travelling like a queen, in state, Pat came
to Dixie. Sixty pounds of sleek Chesapeake Bay, and
a credit to her blood and raising. A bit timid after the
long ride, and, naturally homesick for the farm and
her folks. But, when she found Miss Irma loved her
just as much as she had our own big Pat dog, and that
she had the run of the house and could ride alongside
her mistress and bark out of the car window as loud as
she pleased — why everything became just right. We
took her to our duck club, a comfortable shack alongside a lake full of wildfowl foods and cypress trees.
There she came to know Big and Little Jim and Lelia,
the colored folks who mind the place, and Buck and

Ball, the coonhounds. What a watch dog she became, and what a pet. On hand for a game of "hide me something" the moment we arrived. Some member's slipper to be hunted down, an orange or apple to be pulled off the tall mantel, or a boisterous romp that completely unbedded the dormitory.

At first, Pat was a bit boat shy. I have seen other Chesapeake pups the same way. But before long she found out what such affairs were all about, and thereafter promptly and possessively manned the front over-deck. Her first "duck" was an old boxing glove, about the size of a bird, and of a texture to make her tender mouthed. From the boat, I'd toss the glove far into some tall cover, shoot the gun and bid her "bring!" This process was repeated day after day, and then reversed, the glove being thrown from a blind across open water. Later, a mud hen, caught in a muskrat trap and badly hurt, became Pat's first blood and feathers. Through all Pat's primer days the flight was coming down. Overnight our lake was reloaded with mallards, sprigs, teal, widgeon, shovellers and gadwall.

Opening day, at last! I was shooting that morning with my cousin. Pat evinced a lively interest in everything en route to the blind. When great bunches of quacking mallards leaped as our boat rounded some narrow trail, she squirmed and whined. She had ducks in her blood, all right, and knew there was "something shaking." Looking back at me and my gun, she literally licked her chops. There was that noise due, Pat was figuring. While I waded about placing the "blocks," Pat solemnly inspected each one. But when I weighted and tossed out the first live caller, there was a hullaballoo. In two leaps that sent water flying, she was on top of the shrieking mallard. But a new tone in my shout of "Let it alone," stopped her instantly. Looking straight at me, as though thinking it all out for a moment, she released the struggling drake and marched meekly to the boat. Never again did she pay the slightest attention to a live decoy.

By six forty-five, all was ready. Seven o'clock is "union" shooting hour at our duck club, so a fifteen minute interval of delicious agony had to be endured. Hundreds of ducks, routed from our big pond, returned; the air and water were atwinkle. Pat stationed herself on the boat's prow, just behind the elbow brush. She was strictly at attention. A handsome mallard, our first customer, was just ahead of three more swinging over adjacent timber. We let him glide straight in and alight. The others circled once and dropped in against a faint breeze. These we bagged, and Ev, with his remaining barrel accounted for the original incomer. At the report of our guns I was conscious of Pat's taking a header off her station and buck-jumping toward a flapping bird. She hesitated at first, just as she had done with the poule d'eau, but after a sniff or two, picked up the victim, and with head and tail erect made a perfect retrieve of her first real mallard. Depositing her pick-up, she licked its bedraggled plumage a bit, shook herself furiously, and then smiled up at me. I tossed an empty shell toward a second victim. Instantly she caught the suggestion and was on her way. The sport, from then on, was fast and furious. I let Pat do as she pleased, and she was plenty busy. When time was up she had piled the better part of two limits into the boat. She was a "natural." All that fall her water and wildfowl and gun lessons continued. I used her for geese on the sandbars and had her follow me wading through overflowed timber. Pat made few failures at spotting shot down birds under such acid test. Just before Christmas I shipped her to Marse Henry and wrote him I thought she "had everything" and would retrieve anything that was loose at both ends.

In January, with Pat one year old, I returned to the Potomac for some duck shooting with Marse Henry and Doc. He has his own particular hunting system and methods of working out results. And he gets them, too. He had figured it all out, and reset his blind on the tip of a shore point. To its left, the big river "coves," and a right wind swings up-comers in much closer for stooling. Half a mile or so above, the shallow expanse of Broad Creek lets in, a great rafting place for feeders. Behind the blind a belt of heavy woodland thickens down-shore, into a tangle of low shrubs, vines and beach boulders. Off the abrupt bank, a plank walk extends out to the box, perfectly camouflaged, even down around its ankles, with cedar boughs. Four foot piling allows for tidal variance. Inside are cushioned seats, shell and gun racks, an oil heater for each end, and a heavy tarp cover that can be used as a laprobe to hold in heat during bitter weather. A twelve inch plank, set at just the right angle, catches the wind and tosses it overhead. "I've found out," said Marse Henry, "that in my own home blind I might just as well be reasonably comfortable — we have to do all our own chores around here anyhow, and there is plenty of grief outside the box." Marse Henry is right about that. When you hunt with him you do a man's work somehow or other. There's plenty of room for six gunners and all three of those big Chesapeakes, Fritz, Pat and old Mamma Beck. "Maybe three brown bears is too much of a crowd," continues Marse Henry, "but they're company for me and the Colonel — I like to fool with 'em and watch Beck teach 'em tricks of her trade." Three retrievers in a boat or any other blind than Henry's would be worse than trying to manage four prima donnas in the same opera troupe. But at his place, well, things are just different — even to the actual shooting. Somehow, when the cans rip off from lines winging up-Potomac half a mile out, and make a dart to look you over — you had better make arrangements to do business on a brisk basis. Because, as my old but observing colored friend, Horace Miller, would comment: "dem birds acts so brief." From the jump you might just as well begin at a true forty yards and figure outward. I have shot ducks at many a place and under widely varying conditions, but Marse Henry's is where the diplomas are really handed out. Acquire one there, take 'em as they come, and you can slide up to the firing line at any duck shooting counter in these United States and "take out a stack," feeling reasonably qualified regardless of what you're up against.

That first day there were five of us in the box — Marse Henry, the Colonel, Ira, Doc and I. The Colonel was merely visiting, and Ira was having his gunning helping Doc with the picture machine. I think Pat knew me. She put her paws on my shoulders, stared me straight in the eyes, and grinned. Then she sniffed my jacket carefully, and ended by trying to push me over backwards with face lickings. There was a fine flight, that day. At the crack of our guns, out would bounce all three dogs, with Beck invariably first. Fritz held up his end in good shape, but, to my amazement and chagrin, Pat more or less hung back. With three or four birds down amid wind and wave, three dogs have plenty of work cut out for them. "What's the matter with her," I asked, when several times she held back, or starting rather grudgingly, turned shoreward, "why, you'd think she'd never seen a duck, much less retrieved one." Marse Henry's brow wrinkled. "I don't know," he parried —"I think she's all right basically, or that she'll develop — maybe after your way of shooting down there, she hasn't 'savvied' this deep water stuff — maybe she's depending too much on the old bitch."

But I couldn't exactly figure it out that way. Fritz was out on his own, but all Pat would do was run around in circles. It depressed me terribly after what I'd seen the animal accomplish down home. It was in her, right enough. Why I had pictures of her retrieving, putting ducks into our boat. I could prove it by Harold, or Irma. Harold could tell 'em about that day, for instance, when I banged down a timber scraper that Pat chased clean across the pond and into the big cypress. And on her way back she spotted an overlooked drifter and fetched in a double. And that goose she chased to midriver of the Mississippi and brought in like nobody's business. Something was wrong, somewhere. I grew afraid Marse Henry might think I'd been spoofing him just because Pat was his dog. It wasn't much of a day, on Pat's account. Nor did succeeding shoots prove any more satisfactory. Duck season was running out. I waxed almost morose on the subject of Pat's fall-down. She was alert enough, but compared to the animal I'd worked down home, she apparently didn't know what it was all about. Was Pat yellow? Impossible! Brainless? Certainly not! Why, she was a sweetheart, and smart as a steel trap. Lazy? Not Pat, of all dogs, with that mother of hers, and the stunts I'd seen her pull off. All I could do was wait, and while nature was taking its course, try to puzzle out the thing.

Last day of the wildfowling calendar! One that shook its fist in our faces and flung a dare to do something about it. Offshore, a quarter mile of milling ice; even the steamer channel was fully of heavy floes. Great fields splitting loose from the mouth of Broad Creek and crunching past with a grinding roar that kept us shifting desperately to salvage decoy strings. In-shore the tide-groaning masses piled into towering bergs that fell of their own weight and formed fantastic caves. But our outfit's battle with such elements won and earned its last day's fun. What birds we killed gave Beck a trying time of it. Son Fritz had managed to wire-cut himself and was in the sick bay. Pat was on hand, but of little if any help. She was as affectionate as ever, but somehow palpably shy of it all. Her whole attitude was that of a human being trying, beneath some complex, to grope at the past for spiritual urge.

It was coming good sundown, with first pink and

then a darker gloam mantling Virginia's shore-line. Up and down river distant guns were reluctantly booming hunter's fond farewell to governmental regulation. While Marse Henry and Doc loaded a share of the duffle and birds through the woods copse, I set about battering down the blind's tarpaulin. What a gorgeous after-flare from reflecting ice to sky. "Look your last, you gunners," it seemed to say; "today will soon belong to the log-book — say a prayer for the tomorrow that is hope." An edged wind gnawed at my stiffening fingers. My gun leaned against a snag. Suddenly, down river, across the cove, three shadows blotted a fading patch of ochre east and winked silently our way. Crouching, I snatched my weapon. Black duck! A long way out, but by thunder, I'd have a go at that big center fellow if it was the last shot I ever made.

A dog sprang noiselessly down from the overhead bank and hunkered alongside. I was afraid to take my eyes off the approaching birds. Couldn't be Fritz. A quick, closer scrutiny. Not Beck — her nose and eyebrows were graying. Why — a stabbing blade of hope — it — it — was — Pat. I felt her quiver and heard a faint, eager whine that took me back to sandbars and swamps and boat prows and tall timber. I sensed her lemon eyes ashine, and fixed — with intent to kill. Renewed affection surged through me. This was her game and mine again — together — the kind she'd learned.

No more confinement in the blind — the gun — the game — everything in sight. The complex went glimmering.

A swinging lead, and heavy tubes spat a gash across the wind-whistle. The big center duck tumbled. Beatin the gun, Pat — the real Pat now — lunged — showering me with muddy gravel as she clawed plungingly out onto the ice field. With a fifty yard start, her crippled quarry was fluttering toward the distant open channel and safety. Realization of danger swept over me. Bad business out there — for boat or man — much less a dog. Out where the jam ended, a treacherous coating of shaved snow — and off it relentless floes that would drill a yawl. "Come back, Pat," I yelled, rushing after her until I broke through the crust and into boot-deep eddy. "Pat — Pat — here — here — come back." Far out on the ice a racing dot grew smaller and smaller — lost to sight against distant hills. Then I knew. Seeing me crouched there, it had all swept back to her — images from a dream time. In that brief moment, memory flashed of old Beck's bearing Pat's unborn spirit through icy travail. Men are said to "find themselves." Why not a dog?

And then, as night flung suddenly down, out there among waves and the creaking smash of sullen turmoil, Pat disappeared. Marse Henry was alongside by now, listening to the story and calling, with me, out across the gloom. Fifteen, twenty minutes passed. Our voices hoarsened against the tumult, with something dreadfully pathetic tugging at our hearts. A shred of moonlight tipped the crest of Maryland and swathed the river's shroud with pallid paths. And into its widening beneficence, from behind an ice barrier far to our left, crept an almost ghostly, slow-walking Pat. Pat, grizzly with frozen spray, but, head and tail erect, with a live, unrumpled black duck between her jaws. Marse Henry's eyes and my own met in unutterable relief — and something much, much more. Into our hearts had surged not alone gratitude for Pat's restoration, or a mere coming into her own. Just the choky tribute of silence, a palm from two hard-bitten duck shooters to a dog's flaming courage and unspeakable devotion.

A SHOOTIN' PO' SOUL

WE TOOK our time after shoving off for the south end of old Beaver Dam that morning, its star-crinkled, frosty blackness but forerunner to one of those gloriously beautiful late November days that hunters feel justified in spending to the full. Horace was along in his own double-ender to convoy live decoys, stools and such other "impedimenta" as might hinder Harold's and my enjoyment of the bracing paddle downlake. We made blind, after crashing ice splicings across several lagoons, in a bunch of tall, razor-edged saw grass. Alongside lay an open pond, rimmed by a girdle of willow stumps, and beyond, a wall of steepling cypress.

Stepping gingerly, even in our waders, for the mud was nothing to trifle with, we lifted our boat plump among the whispering reeds. We were perfectly hidden, with our stool spread just right for the suspicion of wind at our backs, and our four live birds, anchored here and there, preening, flapping and calling lustily in sheer exuberance at release among their kind. Overhead, in the dawn, wildfowl began their restless whirr; but Horace, having hidden his pirogue nearby, admonished us that we had a full fifteen minutes before "shooting time." We sat listening. A gang of geese roosting uplake took wing in sudden, clanging uproar — first the muffled beat of wings upon water and then an approaching babble that fetched us the thrill of eager expectancy. But they passed just out of sensible range, a noble chance had they crossed the deadline. How the beggars did honk riverward until their last "E-e-e-ah — Luck-ah-Lonk" died away west.

Our first victim was a high-flying mallard drake craning his snaky head in leery observation on his first and last circle. With a "one may shoot now — eh?" Harold snapped up centering his bird with a pattern of 6s. Down it plunged in a folding wilt, striking jets of ice-spangled spray high across the rose ash of suffusing sunrise.

Thus morning wore itself away. There came shy, high-hat sprigs, with their trim streamlines and illusive drop-in-drop-out tactics. Teal, too, whipping in and out among the stumps, doing amazing stunts while we won or lost gunnery wagers on such feathered pellets. Around noon time, after Horace had emerged from his hiding place, and (to quote the old judge) "gathered up the dead," we saw him disappear toward the big timber. A bit later a squill of smoke came from

[210]

that direction, so we hunted him up and were met with a hail of "I'se gittin' you all sumpin' t' eat!" And, in an aftermath of black coffee and grub, here is the yarn that Horace spun:

"One time t'wuzza gent'man come down t' d' laik wid Mister Hal How'd, so o' cos' Mister Hal sont me wid'im t'see dat he got de proper spote. H'it 'pear, judgin' frum dey cawnversayshun o' de night befo', dat dis gent'man had had him a job on one o' dese he'ah big fightin' botes in som' navy — I he'ah Mister Hal callin' him som' fancy kin'na name. An' Mister Hal done tole me privately dat he had an' still could sto' way 'nuff liquah t'flote de battle ships uv a Nation. Las' thing Mister Hal say t' me was, 'Lissen, Ole Nigger, you watch *yo'sef!*' Whin me an' my man started out he tol' me 'bout how he bin used t' shottin' sixteen inch cannons an' how he sco' fo'teen bulls' eyes frum twelve miles off. I 'lowed das d' kin' eyes dey wuz, too. But whin he tell me dem guns he bin shottin' wuz loaded wid nine hunnard pouns' o' powdah an' dey shots weigh two thousan' poun's I says t' myse'f, I says, '*G-r-e-a-t I—am—*' I says,—'dem guns sho' rambles, don't day, Cap'n?' Den I say t' myse'f I say, 'Uuuu-mmmppphh-huuummpphh—he'ah de very man I bin scared was gwi' show up down he'ah at dis club some day — dis man gwi' kill *all de ducks!*'

"Well, gent'mens, us got all sot in dat bunch o' grass

ovah yonder b'low de Teal Hole. Us 'rived dere long befo' daylite; he say he lak t' commune wid nature. I thow'd out de m'coys. Fin'lly h'it come day an' he'ah rove a bunch o' teals zippin' pas' de Hawg Stan', — right on ovah my man's haid. He peek 'roun' at me an' whisper, 'Whut wuz dat?'

"I say, 'Teals, Cap'n — t-e-e-e-l-s!'

"He say, 'Well, grantin' dey is all you claims dey is, whar d'hell is dey gone?'

"I say, 'Dar dey sits, Major; dar dey is, right outside de grass t'wix' you an' d' m'coys!' Den he see 'em, raise up cautious lak an' take er long aim. Den he pull an' mos' jump in de laik, but de gun don't go off. I he'ah him cuss. I say, 'Cock it, Cap'n, you gotta cock it fus'!' He turn 'roun' an' look kinda foolish. He say, 'Now les' see how dey likes dis — B-l-o-o-m — b-l-o-u-i-e!' But all he done wuz t' thow dem teals up on top uv a wave o' watah an' on off dey went.

"He say, 'Ho'ace,' say, 'das hell ain't it,' say, 't' use er naughtycal 'spression employed by one o' de old instructors,' say, 'my elevashun wuz faulty an' I reckoned wid' out due 'lowance fer magnetic infloonce f' d' law o' giv' an' take.' I say, 'Yaas, suh, h'it sho' stan' t' reason you shot whar dey wuzzn't.' Den I says, kinda concerned lak, I say, 'Commander, maybe yo' fingers done got all col' an' you pulled dem triggers too brief,' I say; 'y' know dem afromatic guns feeds awful fas'.'

He say, 'By jove, Ho'ace,' say, 'you is a rev'lation t' me,' say, 'gret minds uses in d' same channels. You done solv'd d' problem'; say 'he'ah, han' me dat bottle o' Brooklyn Handicap yonder in d' shell bucket.' He hit it a couple o' smacks and say, 'Now den, united us shoots, divided us misses; come on all you ducks — lame, halt, an' blind!'

" 'Bout dat time he'ah come er ol' mallet wid his wings all cupped fixin' t' dive 'mongst d' m'coys. Up riz my man an' holler, 'Dey say d' early bird ketch d' worm but you gwi' ketch — ' B-l-l-a-a-m! Dat ol' drake bounce 'bout fifty foot up in de air an' go off 'bout his bizness, an' my gent'man he cuss an' fume an' scowl an' say, 'Ho'ace,' say, ' 'pon my soul,' say, 'I b'lieves dat stim'lant I jes' took didn' do me no good,' say; 'h'it didn't git mo'n 'bout half way down.' Say, 'han' me dat jimmyjohn,' say, 'I gotta git all dis he'ah kin o' bizness straightened out; dis ain't no way!'

"I giv him de jug an' he rapped it right. He say, 'Ho'ace,' say, 'dat stuff puts a man way ahead o' all his troubles.' An' I say, 'Well, suh, ef such bees d' case I'se runnin' at leas' fo'ty five minits late.' He say, 'O das' right,' say, 'he'ah, boy,' say, 'mek up dat los' time t'wix he'ah an' de nex duck.' I didn' take no chances an' got er little ahead o' d' schedule. I seen right den an' dere dat dat man didn' fear neither fren' n' foe when it come t' swappin' toddies.

"Den, he'ah come er big bunch o' sprigs flutterin' 'cross't d' willers, circlen' low an' fixin' t' settle. I say, "Git raidy, Gen'l!' He say, '*Fo whut?*' I say, 'Gen'l,' I say, 'git raidy.' He say, 'How come all dis he'ah git raidy stuff?' I say, 'sprigs — fixin' t' light out yonder.' He say, 'Are you sho' dey has done 'greed 'mongst dey-seffs t' light?' I say, 'Cap'n, h'its my b'lief dey has.' He say, 'Well, nigger boy, ef das so I sees no pressin' reason why I should fo'ce dey plans t' miscarry.'

"De sprigs dey jes' kerswischet onto de watah, an' gent'mens, I'se he'ah t' state dat som' shootin' *went on.* Up jump d' boss an' up got de ducks. Dat afromatic went t' shootin' an' shot plum out. Nary duck. He grab some shells outa his pocket an' shoot five times mo'. Nuthin' but shootin' an' hollerin' an' cussin'! I says, 'Hol' on, Gen'l!' but, he done runned pool again. He yell out 'Whut's d' matter wid dis dog gonned gun, Ho'ace?' say, 'I kain't stop her'; say, 'he'ah take h'it befo' I throws it in d' laik an' does myse'f some pussonal violence!'—B-l-a-a-a-m—B-l-o-u-i-e——.

"I holler, 'Cap'n, f' goodness sake turn d' thing t' other way, you done got me covered!' Atta'while he set down an' say, 'Ho'ace f' d' life o' me I kain't see how tactics such as dem went on'; say, 'dis ain' no way t' be runnin' no duck shoot'; say, 'gim'me dat flagon, I done tuned up all de nerves but I ain't got d' heart right.' I say t' m'se'f, I say 'Uuummmpphh-

[214]

huummpphh! 'bout d' time you gits d' heart right you gwi' see fo' thousand strange ducks an' six other niggers floatin' roun' dis bote; I wishes I wuz home at d' club settin' round' d' fiah!'

"'Bout den he turn roun' an' say, 'Ho'ace, you's wid me to d' bitter en', ain't you?' I say, 'Cap'n, is dat gun o' yo's whuts lookin' me straight in de face, loaded?' He say, 'You mighty right, ol' nigger,' say, 'h'its jes' ez full o' powdah an' bullets ez patience an' human injunnuity kin stick it.' I say, 'Well, den, Gen'l,' I say, 'I'm wid you long as de ducks flies an' de jug las'. I might ez well be fifty-fifty wid d' boss.' He say, 'Ho'ace,' say, 'how does you handle dese he'ah ducks whut flies so brief dat a man whut shoots frum d'right shoulder kain't do no business wid dem ef' dey comes frum d' other 'rection?' I say, 'Well, Cap'n, you got t' learn t' shoot lak Mister Hal; y' got t' be one o' dem amphibious shooters — one o' dem whut shoots either right or lef' handed.' He turn 'roun an' look at me an' say, 'Ho'ace,' say, 'you don' pack yo' stuff none too well, does you?'

"Den d' ducks started flyin' sho' nuff. He run up d' bote an' down d' bote wid me dodgin' an' twistin' an' pirootin' roun' scan'lous. Fin'lly he say, 'Ho'ace, how many shells has us got lef'?' I say, 'Gen'l dey ain' no mo' in de bucket but you got five in yo' gun.' He say, 'How many is us done shot?' I say, ''Bout fo' hun'-

nard.' 'Bout dat time er ol' mallet flop down out front an' d' Gen'l he up an' turn loose — but on went d' mallet. D' Gen'l start singin', 'Go Stranger — Go Thy Way.' He says, 'Ho'ace,' say, 'we is outa shells an' us is outa luck — take me on t' de house.'

"Dat wuz sho' good news so I pry d' bote outa d' grass an' wuz pushin' out onto d' lake when he'ah drop in a big bunch o' mallets. He jump up t' shoot an' holler, 'Turn d' bote, boy, turn d' bote, he'ah where I gwi' kill d' limit.' I say, 'Don' shoot, Cap'n, don' shoot,' but he yell, 'Turn me — turn me!' — so I set d' paddle in d' mud an' slang d' bote on 'roun'. Well, gent'mens, whut wid d' swing o' dat bote an' him feelin' sorter corruptious, dat afromatic jes' kicked him on outa th' bote an' d' las' thing I seen h'it wuz kickin' him on under an' bubbles wuz risin'. Dey wuzn' nuthin' floatin' 'roun' but some Julia Marlowe seegars. I got me a pocket full o' dem an' den holp him inta d' bote. He open another bottle he had in his bucket an' say, 'Don't ast me who h'it me — take me on to de house an' don't spare d' hosses.'

"Fin'ly I got him to d' house an' change his clos' an' set him up 'long side d' fi'ah. He say, 'Ho'ace, whut kin' o' gun does you shoot?' I say, 'I shoots one o' dem ham'less britch loaders wid infallibus powdah an' dem chilly shots.' He say, 'Whut wuz yo' business befo' you started shootin' ducks an' drinkin' rum fo' yo' livin'?'

I say, 'Cap'n, I wuz er coon hunter.' He say, 'How come you t' quit such a fine night job?' I say, 'H'it come 'bout by gittin' in trouble wid a ha'nt.' He say, 'Wid a w-h-a-a-a-t?' I say, 'Wid a ghos' — a ha'nt.' He say, 'Oh, yes'; say, 'you is one o' dem niggers whut is all de time seein' things. Is h'it a gif' or did you cultivate d' habit?' I say, 'Naw, suh; I jes' natcherl'ly run m'se'f los'.' He say, 'I wanted t' do th' same thing sev'-ul times in my career'; say, 'tell me 'bout it.'

"I say, 'Well, Cap'n, one night whin I wuz livin' ovah in d' hill country 'bout fifty mile frum he'ah I went huntin' one night wid my l'il ole stump-tailed, low, heavy-set dawg name Totelow. Us wuz goin' long mindin' us business whin I thow'd my light up in er tree an' seen two big ole bright eyes shinin' down at me. Den I seen dat I had done shined a tiger coon'. He say, 'What is a tiger coon?' I say, 'Gen'l,' I say, 'd' tiger coon is jes' natcherl'ly d' master coon — he's d' principal man 'mongst d' coons. H'it don' make no diffunce ef h'it be twenty ordinary coons up dat tree ef d' master coon come erlong an' want dat tree all he got t' do is jes' t' let dem other coons know his idea 'bout de matter an' dat settles h'it — dey leaves out. He got fo' mo' stripes 'roun his tail dan d' other coons, he's twice ez big, an' no dawg ain't never lived t' take him wid his boots on. I thow'd up my gun an' whin h'it cracked, why gent'mens, dat tiger coon jes' lep on out o' dat tree an' come on down on me an' Totelow. I dodged an' he landed in de mutton canes, an' Totelow not knowin' no better run in dar an' tied in wid 'im. I ain' nuvver seen n' heard no mo'n de yelp Totelow giv', neither. Den de tiger coon run outa de' bushes an' flewed onto me an' run me up a saplin'. He took his stan' down under dat slim tree an' loll his eyes at me an' cut his tongue out. Fin'lly I 'members er bottle o' Tree Top Tall whut I had in mah pocket, so I took me a swig o' two — h'it wuz gittin' col' hangin' up in dat trees.

"Atta' while I hee'rd a low moanin' soun' away off yonder. H'it come nearer an' nearer, 'till I knowed t' wuz er hunter's horn, but t' wuz d' funnies' soundin' horn ev'h I hee'rd. H'it gimme d' creeps. Den I see'd a light, a blue light creepin' 'crosst de cane tops, an' pretty soon outa d' jungle slips two big ole dawgs. Dey wuz mouse colored wid green tails. No sooner'n de tiger coon see'd dem dawgs n' up de talles' tree he went. Dey jes' set down by dat tree an' wait. De cane open agin' an' out come a raggedy l'il ole man wid long whiskers an' a big horn hung to 'im. He wo' funny lookin' clo's, an' den lookin' hard I seen he had a monkey settin' on his arm. Hadn' none o' dem seed me, so I eas'd annuther swig o' Tree Top Tall inta m'se'f an' keep on lookin'. Dat ole long-whiskered man take d' monkey off his arm an' point up de tree at de tiger coon. Den he giv' de monkey a hick'ry club an' point, an' up

[218]

de tree run de monkey, an' whin de tiger coon seen him
comin' I mean he got in a tur'ble swivet. He run out
to de end uv a big limb an' whin de monkey seen dat he
run up above him, wrop his tail roun' a limb an' swung
down and begin beatin' d' ole tiger coon wid his club.

"Gent'mens, you'all talk about gittin' frailed—why,
he jes' whupped dat coon plum out d' tree. Dem two ole
blue dawgs grabbed him befo' evah he hit de groun' an'
handed him to de ha'nt. He jes' made one grab an'
pulled de hide off an' den bit de carcass in two wid one
bite and thow'd de pieces to de dawgs. Den d' ole man
blow his horn an' de monkey come down and hop up on
his arm. An' 'bout dat time d' ole man look up in de
saplin' an' seen me. I look at him an' seen dat he didn't
have no eyes, jes' places full o' coals o' fi'ah. Right den
my hair riz an' my stummick turned plum ovah an'
outa' dat tree I fell. I landed all in 'mong'st dem dawgs
an' dat ol' man, but gent'mens, I bet I bounced fo' feet
when I hit. I com' to arunnin', an' man-n-n-n-n —
you-all talk 'bout settin' de cane on fi'ah! Well — I
sho' lef' a trail o' smoke behin' me. I runned all night
— an' don't b'lieve I hit de groun' mo'n fo' or five
times. I could hear dat ol' man an' dem dawgs — an'
ev'y now an' den d' ol' man he'd blow dat horn an'
holler — 'Coon death! — coon death!' Sometime
du'in' de early mawnin' I mussa' fell out, fuh whin I
come to I wuz layin' up alongside a big oak lawg back

out yonder whar dat grudge ditch took in. I foun' m' way dis far an' he'ah I bin ev'ah sence — dey tell me h'it mussa bin' fifty miles I runned dat night —"

Horace ceased his tale and applied himself vigorously to a selection from left-over viands. Harold considered our man's story thoughtfully. Then he said: "Horace, I believe that you are unquestionably the biggest liar it has ever been my genuine pleasure to encounter. What else happened to your naval friend who shot the gun with nine hundred pounds of powder and a bullet that weighed two thousand pounds?"

Horace suspended opening operations upon the interior of a pan of browned duck hash. "Well, suh," he said, "y' know, de Commander he had me t' mix him up a long toddy an' den he laid back in his rocker an' says, 'Ho'ace, say, 'us sho' played de wild out yonder dis mawnin', didn' we?' I say, 'Gen'l,' I say, 'you is sho' right — ef' de wild wuz ev'ah played, us done it.' He say, 'Ho'ace,' say, 'de mem'ry o' dis occasion will linger wid me as long, if not longer, as runneth d' mind o' man.' Den he sorter begin t' whimper lak. I say, 'Gen'l,' I say, 'don' cry;' I say, 'I sees lots o' gent'mens miss ducks.' At dat he kin'er perk up an' say, 'Well, deys one thing certain, Ho'ace.' I say, 'whut's dat, Gen'l?' An' he say, 'Well, us sho' missed all de ducks, but deys one thing sure,' say, 'Man-n-n-n — ain' I a shootin' po' soul'?"

THE XIVth OF JOHN

FROM my goose pit on the upper plateau of old Ship Island bar, I used to gaze longingly up and across the tawny Mississippi at a finger-like sand ridge jutting from Arkansas. Under varying water levels my glasses revealed it sometimes as mainland; at others peninsula, or again a mere knob in a blur of dun.

Frequently, that first season, I observed heavy goose traffic avail itself of an apparently unshot landing field. Strange to say, the formation seemed proof against that dismantling to which floods subject river bars. Beyond this barrier, fancy pictured a shallow lagoon, with no telling how many unmolested duck lakes, turkey woods and fur pockets, across the distance of wild Walnut Bend. There must be, I figured, some resistant reef guarding the bar's upper neck; some tight lining to absorb the current rip and eddy suction.

This was years ago. Gas boats were few and far between, though Ed owned a crazy one. Save for stately packets and their stodgier river kin, the only powered craft were occasional steam yachts of the idle rich. To explore that distant goose ground became little short of an obsession.

Taste for adventure had already tempted me to gun the comparatively virgin river territory from which I now visualized greener pastures. With Horace, colored factotum of our duck club, I "made medicine" with a view to invading what promised to be an unspoiled shooting territory. Levees then were not so tall and massive as they are now. Lowlands were practically unlumbered.

At that time, too, there were no goose hunters to amount to anything. I was the reputed and smiled-at "crazy man" who made long wagon drives, lay out nights, or shivered all day in a clammy sand hole waiting for fool geese. The very idea! A few "river rats" took pot shots behind night flares. Once in a while some plantation agent knocked a bird from low flying flocks, or darky croppers successfully stalked cornfield feeders. Wildfowl were shipped openly to city markets. Ours was a made-to-order wilderness. Sixty square miles of dense and varied game haunt. Behind Bordeaux tow-head, lay an old river bed. Its three miles of meander was spotted with hidden ponds, mallard and goose hides de luxe. Just below its reunion with "Ole Miss" we had general headquarters at Ed's house-boat.

No potentate ever governed a more bountiful and carefree domain with less recourse to the mailed fist, than Ed. His rule was the rule of grapevine intelligence raised to Majesty. Illicit river business detoured Ed's landing. Crime met quick detection and fell afoul of sure-fire punishment. Nor did any captain of industry ever finger a wider assortment of apparently aimless but somehow comfortably remunerative enterprises. Ed was steamboat agent, Government lightkeeper, and insurance salesman. He was deputy-sheriff, magistrate, and benign political over-lord. By turns and terms he was gravel and cement manufacturer, portrait painter and critic of national affairs. He dwelt ever upon the brink of some opulent invention.

In addition to activities as ferryman, farmer and amiable usurer, he dealt in fur and cotton. His ventures required no capital save sweat and muscle. They entailed little overhead save space. Losses were minimized on one hand by the grapevine, and on the other by infinite patience. Profits were certified by unhorizoned statutes of limitation, and, if necessary, pistol's point. His talents, as mortician, doubling in white or black, were profound and widely utilized. As chief mourner, orator, residuary legatee, executor with or without bond, referee in local bankruptcy, or umpire out of same, Ed's versatility was astounding. First, last and all the time, however, he was river fisherman, squirrel turner and lazy addict of hound and headlight. Schooled amid the better days of good blood gone to seed, Ed's really poetic and picturesque mentality teemed with original ideas. Smiled at as harmless vagaries, some of them are working soundly today. From loafing intimacy and truant commune with Nature, he had a knack of stealing high lights and shadows, body and soul, from the elements. From his crude studio emerged camera studies as dainty as any fairy theme, or as ruggedly bold as seasons offered. His nets and live boxes fed the sparse countryside with succulent channel-cat, sturgeon, buffalo and gamier fish-bits from inland.

To his office-warehouse, built on high stilts, the black folks came afoot and mule-back for barter and counsel in wedlock or its later sundering. By powers in him legally vested, Ed tied conjugal knots in ceremony and language all his own. For marriage certificates he used the bills of lading of his steamboat line. I can see him now, handing them out with much ado as to official signature, seal, blotting and fee taking. The important, last-named detail secured, it was his custom to tender the impending litigants a choice catfish as wedding gift. Divorce proceedings revealed similar recourse to originality. As insurance factor in multifold phases of the risk, Ed had accumulated a safe full of expired or cancelled fire policies. Couples

arriving wordily or riotously at dissolution of the banns
and bonds, were summonsed via the grapevine, and
hustled unceremoniously before the Squire. Impartial
offices of divorce proctorship failing, Ed gravely and
sorrowfully produced two gaudy and important looking documents. He then lectured the assembled dispu-
tants and combatants upon the evils and excessive
financial depletions born of connubial litigation. Followed solemnly attested signatures (or more likely
mark-making) and fees of such calamitous ravage as
to border forcible extraction from the body. The now
thoroughly subdued parties of all parts drew off; emo-
tional in the possession of dearly bought freedom; but
headed soon for "bill-of-lading" remating in newer
fields. Kindly, fearless Ed! Gone, long since. Billeted
in an ante-bellum graveyard behind the levee, with his
friendly enemy, Old Man River. Asleep at the bole
of a gnarled cypress, where all who pass that nigh forgotten way linger to leave the friendly words and kind
thoughts they have of him. He's somewhere around
though; count on that. No doubt in one of "the many
mansions that are in my Father's house." But for happiness, old Ed didn't really need a mansion.

Toward the fag end of the shooting season the river
usually reached its higher stage. With its first tell-tale
litter of brushy driftage and foam sponge, water
smashed through our old river. Its bed of willows, rank

weeds and grasses became a duck paradise. From dawn to dusk, sinuous ribbons of wild fowl poured above its crescent. When the cut-off became too deep to wade, we poled across in Ed's skiff and hunted along this backwater. We had every dangerous step-off spotted and knew well enough when to take the current seriously. For all his familiarity, Ed cherished a vast respect for the Father of Waters. His commodious houseboat was blocked up in a bank clearing from which dangerous timber had been felled against the coming of a twister. But when high-water was receding rapidly, his entire household lived more or less in mortal terror of caving banks.

"I 'member one time in per'tic'ler," Ed used to relate around our camp fire, while an obnoxious corn-cob pipe fumed like a condemned fertilizer plant; "T'wuz daid o' night, but the ol' lady wuz up. We all wuz, pretty much, com' t' think of it. Anyways, th' ol' woman wuz glandin' a coon I'd ketched. Naw she warn't, neither; she wuz presarvin' som' muscadines— a failin' o' mine — them muscadines. But, all of a sudden, it com' a sorta 'queswishit.' I felt th' ol' boat kinda shiver an' then go t' slippin' an' slidin'. Yup! y'betcha' I knowed whut had done took place. O' co'se h'it scairt th' livin' whey outa me, but I run to th' back do'h — I wuz atrimmin' m' corns at th' moment — an' befo' Gawd an' m' countrymen, 'bout half a acre o' ou'h front yard wuz easin' inta th' river, an' us along with h'it. Things wuz sho' goin' down hill, but, gent'mens, she hit th' watah on an even keel an' bounced a time or two on th' backwash befo' she set still. I knowed her chinks wuz tight; so I yells to th' oldes' boy, I says, 'Leave off bellerin',' I says, 'an' help yo' Ma hol' them hot muscadines onta th' stove.' Then I made th' second kid grab a pike-pole. 'Quit bawlin',' I says to him, 'she'll float; quit tryin' t' pull them breeches on back-'uds,' I says, 'an' go t' shovin'.' Well, we lined her back inta th' eddy, an' in a day or so th' nex' rise lifted us back out onta new bank. Naw, suh; naw, suh; nuv'ah los' a single darn thing. Le's see, though. Yup, that no 'count, egg-bustin' coon dawg I had then, did go ov'-bode. I wish he'd a stayed thar, too. That sapsucker couldn't track an el'phunt across a three acre field with its throat cut frum ear to ear an' three foot o' snow on th' groun'. But, outside o' that, thar warn't no per'tic'-ler goins' on — didn' even wake up th' younges' baby."

Finally, we planned the raid. "De bes' way t' git dar," allowed Horace, "is to borry Mister Ed's skifft, an' git er real early start. Ax him t' leave de bote at de haid o' de inside chute — us kin walk dat far. Den, us pulls up pas' de Whitehall place 'bout two miles, an' shoots cross't wid de current swingin' us back whar us bound. Dat evenin' us comes back easy, driffin' all de way down an' lan' at Mister Ed's."

It meant a battle. In my mind's eye I rechecked every foot of the route. But because of the birds I'd watched use the place, getting there would be worth any hardship. "Ride over Sunday and ask Mister Ed to leave us the boat," I instructed; "I'll come down Monday evening and we'll tackle the job on Tuesday." Horace and I met to arrange final details. The boat, with two sets of sweeps, was reported ready. Two sacks of wooden goose profiles, a stubby shovel, and my shoulder pack were loaded into the light buggy. In addition to tea bucket and iron rations, the bag held camera, binoculars, 10 gauge 2's for my big double, and similar ammunition for the 12 bore loaned to Horace, as gun bearer. Weather prognostication gave reasonable assurance of co-operation by the elements.

A sketchy breakfast was behind me at two thirty next morning. Horace picked up the reins; gave Red Fox, our tall-stepping mule, the watchword and we were off. Stabling our rig in the lee of Ed's sleeping domicile, we shouldered the load, hit a familiar trail for thirty minutes and dumped things into the waiting skiff. After ten minutes paddling, we nosed gradually out to swifter contact with the great adventure. Stripped to rowing comfort, we warmed to the raw job. We were bucking the upper reach of a great reversed "S," with two miles hard lifting behind, when a packet rounded Walnut Bend. Knowing the danger of being

The Author on a goose bar

Ho'ace enjoying himself

caught in the dark too close betwixt wave wash and steep, caving bank, we landed and yanked out. The panting monster churned past so close we could see her "rousters" lying about decks, and hear the leadman chanting his fathoms. Looking after her while the waves broke, we sighted a second steamer coming up the river, but apparently well down, giving us ample time to cross. We shoved off and bent silently to the oars. The weather had thickened. We were making good headway, and nearing mid-channel.

"Gawdamighty, Mister Nash," suddenly exclaimed Horace, "dat big bote is shovin' blind barges — ain' no lights ahead — an' us is right in dey path." Resting on my oar, I swung about. One glance told the truth. There she was, and out front, with no vestige of warning, a long line of false space and deadly black hulks angling directly at us. Too late to turn back or dodge. The current dragged like a giant magnet. Just one chance on earth — beat her across the line of collision. "Horace," I said, as evenly as I could, "strike some matches and wave 'em — they might see, and slow down — then pull to beat hell."

Brains and a sense of propriety never lacked in Horace. A pinpoint of light flared and died. Meanwhile, with everything in me slowly congealing, I tried to hold on our course, without looking. With a grunt, Horace picked up the stroke. We leaped forward. An upthrusting black wall protruded into our eye corners. Suddenly the tow boat's engines shut down. They had caught the warning. In the stillness a louder rush of churning water flogged our ears. It was going to be deadly close. A long-forgotten numbness crept into my forearms. Today's slow-motion dream films hopped madly past an imperiled brain awaiting the crash and oblivion. I saw our baby's tiny new face peeping up at me from blankets and crib, and Irma's rapt gaze. Then —somehow—I was number two again in a Weld crew. Cold dusk stippling the jumpy Charles river basin — a boatload of freshmen battling for jobs with Johnny Harvard — megaphoned voices bellowing from the launch — the Old Man himself — altogether now! The baby's face again. We've got to win — that's it — come on now you — pick it up number two — that's it — feather-wrists-catch — legs-drive — huunnh — drive — ! We rise to meet a smashing crest — hang suspended — tilt — dip crazily, and are slapped side-winding from beneath the tow's prow as it crunches past. Half sinking, we fall slowly aside, Horace bailing desperately with his hat. Lantern in hand, a deck-dauber races to the side rail and roars curses. Reviving somewhat, I suspend operations to send back worse. A searchlight pries from the pilot house and holds us for a second. Engines throb, and she is back on her deadly, unthinking way.

We had drifted badly during the bailing process and found ourselves considerably below the objective. In twenty minutes, however, we sneaked around the bar's comb and into dead water. Half a mile's easy passage along the reef took us to its base, and from these shallows roared a mass of roosting ducks and geese. Apparently we had hit the spot. "Is you still got dat l'il phial o' Frinch brandy I bin seein' you carry fo' so long, Mister Nash?" Horace had a memory. "T'wuz in yo' sack las' week, de bottle Mister Tim O'Sullivan giv' you an' you ain't nevah even opened?" There was a note of personal injury in the darky's tone. "Yes," I replied, "and what's more here is where it gets opened and worked on, too." I took a hearty swig of the rare, courage-building fluid, and suggested that Horace pour himself a smile. He met the proposal with what amounted to a broad grin, that aroused my admiration if not downright apprehension. "Mistah Nash," he reproached, "I ain' nevah befo' in dis life seed you tamper wid de Demon Rum." "Well," I affirmed, "I hope never to have better occasion for use of another." And Horace added, "Ain't it de trufe, Cap'n!"

Still a bit unstrung, we hoisted the outfit, pegged the boat and set out to explore. A hint of dawn smudged the East. Climbing to the backbone of the bar, we crossed its neck, looking for both goose and human tracks. Not a trace of the latter, but plenty of paddle marks and sign. We dug in at dead center of the open bar—twenty minutes spelling, with the off-man setting up the shadows. Our pits were thirty yards apart, with a southwest breeze fanning the backs of our necks and the decoys leading back into the hollow square of a death-trap pocket. Our first customers came from down river and the home bar. Their penciled line, looming abruptly against half light, mounted the plateau, saw our gang, pitched and broke into a gaggle of conversation. To this day I believe our profiles were the first to take toll from that sand spit. Then our visitors ceased talking and sailed straight in with a roar of wing-whiffs and back-peddling. They were through the opening and shin dropping when my first swath of twos mowed down a lapped pair and raked a third skimming not three feet from the sand. With birds massed heavily over him by this blast, Horace stood up in his pit and carefully pulled down a fourth. Hardly had we retrieved the slain when from over the woods behind us, evidently coming from some roost lake, swooped a second flock. One almost unsuspicious circle and in they rushed. Three stayed behind. Business quieted temporarily. Meanwhile burly dark clouds ran the oncoming sun out of business. The wind freshened. Flock after flock of geese traded up-river. Shots at one lot frequently scared off another bunch attempting to make our position. Of such flights are goose hunters' dreams made. But, with sixteen down and two "crips" in the river, we called it a day as far as the honkers were concerned. There was no bag limit in those days, but even then I did have a reasonable conscience, and game was appreciated and eaten at home and by neighbors. Few times have I ever seen opportunity as propitious for actual slaughter. It was coming noon. Time to eat a bite, and do some "roustabouting" in the tall and uncut. It required two trips to lower the scenery and stow it, geese and all, in the tub. Horace boiled the "kittle" in a clump of willows. We counted any number of flocks still coming to the bar while we lay there munching sandwiches. My pre-season obsession had struck pay dirt.

Investigation inland revealed a promised-land of sport. Within a quarter of a mile, but too far off for a shot, we flushed a spread of wild turkeys. Farther on, hidden among the cotton woods and willows off the main bar, we came upon a shallow, stumpy lake literally alive with undisturbed mallards, teal and sprig. What a sight it was, and all ours for the shooting. We put them up and out without firing a shot. Then, while skies darkened, I called from the bank and soon got down an even dozen from returning drakes and hens. It was well past mid-afternoon when, heavily laden, we lunged from the rank undergrowth and flung our bag into the boat. By now we had a load in that craft, too. A half gale had risen. Sand spouts whirled over-head, off the bar. The lagoon was comparatively quiet, but the river beyond was a mass of seething whitecaps. Once past the rim's protection, we would have things coming our way and be in for trouble aplenty. That we knew full well, for up-current wind blows a heavy double chop. After the morning's fright, however, neither of us had much stomach for more trouble. A full two miles of it lay dead ahead once we cut the point.

"Sho' looks bad, Mistah Nash," opined Horace, "you reckon us kin mek h'it — mebbe us better try to mek de other bar fus' an' walk on home — I'd ruther mek fo' trips walkin' dan one swimmin'—tell you de trufe, Cap'n, I done jes' natcherly los' my taste fo' dis river—I wants t' keep de groun' under my feets—ef I uvah gits h'it dar agin'."

"It may get worse," I countered, "let's get going."

Carefully adjusting the ballast to throw the boat's nose high, we held to the bar's lee and then, forced to, shot from cover. Instantly we bucked a slogging welter. Three minutes later we had lost all count of time and distance. Wind gouged and waves battered. It was drawing dusk. Showers of spray and water sloshing my ankles soon told their own uneasy story. "Cap'n," stuttered Horace, "dis bote is gittin' logy." We were taking a bad beating. Just then I caught the wind-blown "pop-

poppety-pop" of a gas engine. As we leaped from a wave trough I had a flash of old Ed's big fishing yawl careening a circle through the gloom. Then a rain squall blotted salvation from sight. Horace yelled encouragement. Up to us curved the rescue boat, and Ed, an oil-skinned, bareheaded helmsman, hurled a hissing rope over Horace's clawing arms. It was doubled close up in jig time, and half an hour later we were fast to the dock. Ed practically made history of the French brandy, and his rising pæans of praise followed us as we swung off into the night. Up the road a piece, a newly thrown tree forced us into a detour that only Red Fox's sixth sense plucked from the pitchy darkness. With unerring instinct the mule entered the gap and stopped.

"Lemme light a cig'rette, please, suh," said Horace.

I don't know why, but I raised a warding hand. Red Fox made a half step. My guarding palm struck and closed about a fang of cold barbed-wire. Even as I yelled "w-h-o-a" it sank in and snagged. Horace gave a cry of startled pain. Red Fox stopped. We backed off and struck a light. My right palm was punctured and torn. Horace had a two inch rip across his throat. Some negro tenant, moving into a cabin nearby, had carelessly left a wire hanging.

I did ample justice to the worthy repast that Molly had waiting. Horace's voice, mouthy from his own contact with ample victuals, floated from the kitchen:

"Mighty nigh runned ovah by de bote—putty much drownded in de storm—an' m' th'oat almos' cut in two 'gin'st de bob-wire." Molly groaned in sympathy, and spoke from the doorway, "Cap'n, you sho' gwi' say yo' prayers dis night, ain' you?"

All alone I entered the club room to ponder things there. Before long Horace entered. Standing beneath the swinging lamp, he shook out his "specs" and opened a dog-eared Bible. Now I see the bulk of him, silhouetted against a dim background of gun lockers, shell boxes and stacked decoys. Finding his place and lowering the book, he said: "Mistah Nash, whin dat bote wuz fixin' t' fly all ovah us, does you know de fus' thing I thought about? Well, suh, t'wuz dat l'il new baby at yo' hous'—an—an'—po' Miss Irma."

I ceased smiling at an anticipated sermon. We used to have them nights, everything from spiritualism to Daniel in the lion's den. How he had plumbed my own poor thoughts.

"Y' know, suh," he continued gravely, "I knows Gawd's word f'm' kiver t' kiver, but mah favorite Gospel is de Fo'teenth o' St. Jawn. He'ah t'is now, suh." As he tossed back his head to focus a reading point, the iodined throat gash was brought into vivid relief. He smiled aside at me. "Whin I see'd dis mawnin' how near to death us wuz, I begin' repeatin' t' m' sef—I say—'Let not yo' heart be troubled; ye b'lieves in Gawd, b'lieve also in ME. In my Father's house are many mansions; if it were not so, I would hav' tol' you'."

Somehow I couldn't look up. The silver loyalty and golden faith of it all suddenly brought moisture to unstrung eyelids. The lamplight suddenly misted a trifle. On and on droned the darky's humble Te Deum through St. John. "I am the way, and the truth, and the Life," he chanted, almost in exaltation; "no man cometh unto the Father, but by ME'." I managed to steady and look again. Horace was saying; "I had done prayed t' my'sef — down t' verse thirteen — whin I heer'd dem waves arushin' off'n de barge bote; so, I say —'Lawd,' I says, 'whut YOU tells us is—"Whatsoever ye shall ask in MY name, dat will I do." Den, as you 'members, suh, com' dat bigges' wave an' flammed us right on out de way o' death."

There was triumph in the negro's voice. He closed his Bible, and said, almost musingly, "Ef ye shall ask ennything in MY name, I will do it." Turning toward the doorway, he added gently: "An' whin us wuz millin' roun' out dar 'mong'st all dem wild wat'ahs an' de darkness, I skipped on down t' verse eighteen, whar HE say—'I will not leave you comfortless; I will come to you.' An' den, suh, I looked up thu' all dem roahin' winds an' rain, an' sho-nuff he'ah com' ol' Mister Ed's bote."

[237]

Maybe Horace thought I was just tired, or inattentive, but I wasn't. From clock-winding, he asked: "Does us shoot in de Teal Hol' in de mawnin'?" Fighting something out of my voice, I replied, turning out the lamp—"Yes—the Teal Hole ought to be a good shoot on this wind—if it holds. Good night—and thank you kindly—Horace."

What fired this train of reflection was the marriage of my daughter—the baby. I realize now that the average duck-shooting Dad undergoes no end of self examination as the moment nears for a one and only duckling to spread young wings for the mating migration. So, when the organ pealed its summons and the bride and I stepped off down the long aisle, I was wishing that old Horace could be among the family servants and colored friends I noted in the pews reserved for them. Two of them had spanked me as an urchin. Up front I spotted two or three goose hunters, odd looking in their wedding scenery.

A few moments later, I had "given this woman" in marriage and retired to Irma's consoling presence. It was, it always is, and ever shall be beautiful, this plighting of troth, sealed in Youth's perfect adoration. A wave of flowering incense off innocence! A vast organ pulsating soft allure to faiths exchanged. Somehow, though, I found myself peering through something away back yonder—at the murk of a dark river-death clutching in the offing. At a tiny face peeping up through pink blankets—at a mother's radiant smile. Then, as swiftly, dusk again—the Charles river basin —the Old Man's voice—and coxey's too—legs-drive-feather-catch-voices lost in the roar of an engulfing wash—numb wrists—whitecaps—old Ed's white mane atoss—the hissing rope's end!

Odd, how thoughts go racing. A peaceful corner of Beaver Dam, in bream fishing time. Flowering willows. May-pops. Horace baiting baby's hook, and crying amid vast excitement, "Hol' im, chile, hol' im," as the little thing clings grimly to sawing cane, with line swishing frantically through sun flecked waters. Good old Horace. But for him—perhaps—

The vague mist thickens. There he is again, against the lamplight, thumbing his old, dog-eared Bible. "De fus' thing I thought 'bout, wuz' dat l'il new baby—an' po' Miss Irma." Why! that's the baby up there now—safe and sound!

Horace's voice again: "The Fo'teenth o' Jawn— 'Let not yo' heart be troubled—where I am, there ye may be also—the way, and the truth, and the Life—whatsoever ye may ask in My name—I will come to you'."

The mist is all too thick now—the old sandbar—recurring melody from files of geese—dwindling—lost—lost through the years.

Recessional boomed. I must have been dreaming, it must be time to pick up. Sundown and dreams. No! For there was Irma, patting my hand and smiling the dear old message up at me through wet, joyous eyes. Surely I had been listening to SOME ONE. And now —I KNOW.